From the Files of

Madison Finn

Read all the books about Madison Finn!

Don't miss the Super Editions:

From the Files of

Madison Finn

Super Edition #3:
Friends till the End

By Laura Dower

HYPERION
New York

Text copyright © 2007 by Laura Dower

From the Files of Madison Finn is a registered trademark of Disney Enterprises, Inc.

All rights reserved. No part of this book may be reproduced or transmitted in any form or by any means, electronic or mechanical, including photo-copying, recording, or by any information storage and retrieval system, without written permission from the publisher. For information address Hyperion Paperbacks for Children, 114 Fifth Avenue, New York, New York 10011-5690.

Printed in the United States of America

First Edition
1 3 5 7 9 10 8 6 4 2

The main body of text of this book is set in 11.5-point Frutiger Roman.

ISBN-13: 978-1-4231-0223-6
ISBN-10: 1-4231-0223-1

Visit www.hyperionbooksforchildren.com

This one's for you, Helen, with thanks and love for the long, groovy ride.

A special shout-out to all the copy editors, proofreaders, Colin Hosten, Karen Hudson, and (of course) the fans.

Far Hills Junior High School

Dear Parents,

Congratulations! Your son or daughter has successfully made it through the school year at Far Hills. Whether he or she will be moving up to the next class at Far Hills Junior High or graduating and moving on to high school, this is an exciting time for you to share in his or her achievements. We have planned several activities to mark the occasion.

In addition to the two moving-up ceremonies for students in classes seven and eight, we will be hosting a formal graduation for all ninth graders. A limited number of tickets are available for all of these events. Please contact the school office for further details. Take note of the following important dates:

Wednesday, June 21
• FHJH Annual Musical Revue (all classes), 7 p.m.

Thursday, June 22
• Moving-Up Ceremonies for 7th and 8th Grade, 10 a.m.
• Academic and Sports Awards (Both Classes), 11 a.m.
• School Buffet, 12 p.m.

Call everyone about family party!

Friday, June 23 (Note: only ninth graders need attend)
• Graduation Day Ceremony with Guest Speaker, 10 a.m.
• Barbecue and Games on South Lawn, 11:30 a.m.

Thank you for all of your support throughout the school year. We are proud to call each student—and you—a member of the Far Hills family. We wish you and yours a bright future.

Sincerely,
Principal Joe Bernard
Assistant Principal Bonnie Goode

Chapter 1

"What are you looking at?" Madison asked, giving Egg the evil eye.

She quickly placed her hands over the screen to block Egg's view. Did he have to sit *that* close? What was his problem? Madison had opened a browser to check her e-mail on bigfishbowl.com. The last person she wanted to have see her private e-mail was Walter Diaz, otherwise known as Egg.

Making a face, Egg snapped back. "Mrs. Wing would fail you if she knew how much you do that."

"Do *what*?" Madison asked, glancing toward the front of the computer lab, where Mrs. Wing was talking to another student.

"You know," Egg said. "Pretend to do real work. I can see under your hand. That's e-mail, isn't it?"

"Hmph!" Madison grumbled.

Egg raised his eyebrows. "So it's okay to be on your own Web site half the time, when you should be updating the school site," he said. "The only time you do any real work in here is when *she* stands over your shoulder."

Madison bit her lip. "Wh—wh—what?" she stammered. Of course, there was a bit of truth in what he said, but she wasn't about to admit that.

Egg rolled his eyes. "Wh—wh—whatever," he said, mimicking her. Laughing to himself, he turned back to his computer. He knew how to push all of Madison's buttons.

Madison knew she took *some* liberties in the computer lab. Egg was right about that. But she only went online to do personal stuff when she had already finished her homework and class assignments.

Egg sat back, still still chuckling.

Was he just pulling her leg? Or was he really threatening to tattle to Mrs. Wing? No fair! Egg was the one who always goofed around and never turned in his computer homework on time. He was actually the smartest kid in the whole class, but he never acted like it.

Squinch!

Madison jumped up and lunged for Egg's arm. Her fingers pinched his shoulder—hard.

"You stink," she growled, sounding like her pug, Phineas T. Finn.

"Ouch!" Egg said, pushing his chair back. "Get away from me."

Madison laughed to herself. She wasn't trying to be mean, of course. This was just how she and Egg communicated sometimes. They were like brother and sister—with fangs and claws.

Mrs. Wing turned toward their desks. So Madison and Egg put a lid on the quarrel. They knew how to keep quiet when it mattered, and now was definitely one of those times.

When Mrs. Wing seemed satisfied that nothing funny was going on, she glanced away. Egg made a sourpuss face at Madison.

"Nice going, Maddie," Egg said.

Then he moved his chair away from her desk and closer to the desk of his friend, Drew, on the other side of the computer terminal.

Madison huffed. Could Egg be any more annoying? She poked again at her own computer keys, pretending to get back to real work, but it was no use. After ten seconds, she gave up. She was way too distracted, and class was practically over anyway. Well, halfway over, at least.

The end of the school year was approaching fast, and it was getting harder and harder to focus on anything except the promise of beach days, fireworks, and (fingers crossed) summer crushes. Madison's mind had gotten very good at wandering. These days, she had the sustained concentration of a gnat.

She wasn't alone, of course. Ever since the beginning of June, there wasn't a seventh, eighth, or ninth grader in the building who was able to concentrate on his or her schoolwork. How could anyone? The color of the sky had turned a hypnotic, clear blue. Teeny purple and yellow and orange flowers bloomed at the edges of the Far Hills fields.

Each afternoon for the last week, Madison and her BFFs had spent time out in front of the school, lying on the lawn. All of them, Madison included, wanted desperately to embrace the air under warm sunbeams, arms outstretched and toes wriggling in trendy new sandals.

At least a *part* of Madison wanted all that.

Then there was the other part of Madison; the part that was super freaked out about the end of the school year; the part that wanted to hide out in a closet. This was the part of her that couldn't bear to think about the prospect of life without her seventh-grade teachers—or anyone else from school, for that matter. Summers had come and gone before, but now seventh grade was really (and truly) ending. Everything felt so drop-dead final, and Madison hated goodbyes. So today Madison wanted to pretend nothing was going to change. She wanted to stay right here in this seventh-grade class with her closest friends.

Mrs. Wing hustled from computer station to computer station, continuing her typical class rounds. She paused at student terminals, checked classwork,

4

and chatted about new software applications with the most enthusiastic students. Madison watched as Mrs. Wing bent and stretched, laughed and talked, waving her arms in the air so her bracelets jangled. The thought of being in any computer class *without* someone as nice (and as good a dresser) as Mrs. Wing made Madison's stomach flip. What would the eighth-grade computer cybrarian be like?

"Okay, everyone," Mrs. Wing said, striding back to the center of the lab after about twenty minutes. She clapped loudly to get everyone's attention. "We have half of class remaining . . . and plenty of work to be done."

"More work?" Egg asked, keeping his voice low. "Is she kidding? Why do *we* always get stuck with the work? The other computer class has been playing games all week."

"Yeah," Madison let out her own deep, confused sigh. "Figures," she mumbled, not wanting to do any work, either.

Undeterred by her students' apparent lack of enthusiasm, Mrs. Wing powered up a laptop with a projector at the front of the classroom and showed the students exactly what kind of work they would be doing.

It was a special project for the end of the school year.

But it actually looked *fun*.

"Every year, students create individual pages on

5

the Web," Mrs. Wing explained. "We call these memory pages. They get posted on the school site."

"What do you put on a memory page?" a girl asked.

"Well . . ." Mrs. Wing started to say, but then she was interrupted by Lance, a boy in seventh grade who loved to answer questions but who usually had the wrong answer. "Uh . . . what if I have a *bad* memory?" he asked. "Does that mean I have to do a bad memory page?"

Everyone chuckled at that remark, including Mrs. Wing.

"Well," Mrs. Wing went on, "I have a feeling you won't have that problem, Lance. Anything goes on these pages. You just have to put down simple memories from seventh grade. For example . . . a student can write about his or her sports team, or a positive recollection about a teacher . . ."

"Like *you*," Madison chimed in, smiling.

Mrs. Wing threw up her arms, and her bangles jangled again. "Why, thank you, Madison," she replied with a wink. "That would be nice."

As Mrs. Wing clicked a key on her computer, a sample memory page came into view on the board. At the top was a ribbon-edged border. There was room for a photograph. A student's name appeared in bold capital letters across the top.

"Wait a minute," Lance asked aloud. "Who's Johnny Somebody? Is he in our class?"

"That's obviously a made-up name, you dork," Egg said.

"Mr. Diaz . . ."

Madison was sure Mrs. Wing was about to reprimand Egg for making a rude remark in the middle of class, when Drew snorted—loudly. The snort sent the whole class into hysterics.

"Class, *class*," Mrs. Wing cautioned them in a stern voice. "You are some of my brightest students, and I really need your help today—and for the remainder of the school year. So, let's please focus on the project at hand. *Please*. And that goes triple for you, Mr. Diaz, thank *you* very much."

Madison laughed to herself. There was nothing like watching her friend Egg be scolded like that by a teacher. It usually meant he didn't say anything else for at least ten minutes.

The Web screen shots Mrs. Wing projected from her computer up onto the board were way more exciting than Madison or any of the other students could have imagined. Colorful, interactive borders framed photos and words. She displayed not only the memory pages, but also the newly updated Web pages about the school year overall: pages that had been designed by her and another computer teacher, who taught ninth grade. The look of the FHJH Web site had gone from basic to bold in nine months. Madison smiled. She was proud to have been a part of all that.

Each memory page featured a string of questions about school life. Next to each question was a blank line. Each student's answers appeared on his or her Web page. At the very bottom was a space to write a longer message.

As they sat there watching the demonstration, Madison began to feel a twinge in her gut. Was it nerves? Or had she forgotten to eat enough lunch? Madison knew the truth: the feelings had to do with MUD, aka Moving Up Day. What else could it be?

When the demonstration concluded, Madison reached for her orange bag, which she'd dropped on the floor between her desk and Egg's. As she grabbed it, a notebook fell out of the bag. And then, a folded piece of paper slipped out of the notebook.

Madison scrambled to get up from the chair and snatch the paper back, but she wasn't fast enough. Egg got to it first.

"What's *this*?" Egg asked, dangling it in the air near Madison's head.

"Give it back," Madison demanded.

"Who handwrites notes anymore?" Drew asked teasingly. "Principal Bernard?"

"Very funny," Madison said. She felt her cheeks burn. "This is *so* none of your business," she snarled.

But it was too late. Egg already had the note open. *"Dear Finnster,"* he said, reading aloud.

Madison cringed. The identity of the note's author was obvious: Hart Jones, Madison's on-again, off-again, and now permanently on seventh-grade crush. Finnster was his special nickname for her, and everyone knew it. Thankfully, he was *not* in the classroom.

"Hart wrote you a note?" Egg cried. "What a drip."

"He is not!" cried Madison.

"Dear Finnster," Egg continued reading. *"I can get my dad to drive us to the movies on Sunday. Can you come? LMK, Hart."*

"LMK? What's that?" Drew asked.

"Let me know," Madison said firmly.

"Why didn't he write, *love*, Hart?" Egg asked, letting out a huge guffaw.

Predictably, Drew snorted at Egg's comment.

Mrs. Wing heard the fuss. "What's the problem over here, boys?" she asked, striding over, hands on her hips.

Egg crumpled the note in his fist and pretended nothing was going on. Drew kept silent. Madison felt too awkward to say a word.

Luckily for all of them, the bell rang out. Class was over. Egg opened his fist and tossed the note back at Madison.

"Sorry," he grumbled, picking up his bag.

Madison pasted on a fake smile. "Sure," she said, shuffling toward the classroom door.

Mrs. Wing called out from behind her desk, "Don't forget! Tomorrow we will start inputting memory pages and fine-tuning the site together. And in addition to posting everyone else's Web memory pages, you will have to write a Web page of your own. Think about what you want to say. It's your seventh-grade legacy, after all. . . ."

Madison and the rest of the class moved quickly out into the hall. She ducked into a stairwell, opened her orange bag, and plucked out her cell phone.

No text messages.

What a disaster. If only Hart had not sent her that handwritten note. If he'd text-messaged her instead, then no one—least of all Egg—would have been able to read it.

Grrrrrrr.

After the second bell, Madison dashed out of the stairwell and headed for Mr. Danehy's science class. Crowds of students changing classes in the hallway made the short walk feel like riding in a bumper car. Madison nearly lost her footing twice.

Posted on the walls in the hallway near Mr. Danehy's room Madison spotted a row of cool posters promoting the upcoming events at school. One of the main events advertised was the first Friday meeting for the musical revue. At the top of the poster, the words *Are You Musical?* shed light on one of Madison's end-of-year issues. How could someone as completely *un*musical as she was participate in a song-and-dance show?

Her eyes lingered on the poster. The harder

Madison thought about getting onstage and singing or dancing or *both* (aaaagh!), the harder she tapped her foot on the ground anxiously.

Just then, someone walked up to her.

"School revue," a voice said. "I am so psyched."

Madison turned to see her nemesis, Ivy Daly, otherwise known as Poison Ivy. The enemy was decked out in a sundress with flowers along the hem.

"Are you doing the revue, too?" Madison asked Ivy.

"Of course," Ivy replied.

"I wasn't sure. . . ."

"*You're* not doing the revue, are you?" Ivy asked, rolling her eyes.

Madison turned and glared. "Why shouldn't I?"

Ivy pretended to stifle a laugh. "You know . . . hey . . . you're not exactly a performer now, are you? I mean, you practically fall apart onstage. . . ."

"What are you talking about?" Madison asked. "I can do the revue if I want. I can do anything—and everything—I want."

"Wow, school's almost over, and you still don't get it, do you?" Ivy sighed, slinging her pink metallic bag over her shoulder.

"Don't get what?" Madison asked, genuinely baffled.

Ivy fluttered her lashes. "You keep trying and trying, but you'll never, ever be the class star," Ivy said smugly. "Um . . . that position's already been filled."

And with that, Ivy turned on her heel and smoothly walked into Mr. Danehy's room.

At that moment, with other kids elbowing past and the poster still asking *Are You Musical?*, Madison knew what she had to do. Not only would she sign up to be a part of the revue, but she would do everything in her power to show Ivy Daly—once and for all—who the better of the two of them was.

The problem? She only had until the end of seventh grade to do it.

Chapter 2

"There are going to be a few changes around here," Mr. Danehy announced boldly at the start of class. His eyes twinkled when he said it, too, which made it seem all the more genuine. "First of all, there will be no more long, tedious reading assignments."

"Cool!" someone said. The rest of the class let out a collective sigh of relief.

"Second, you can come to class late if you want. I understand," Mr. Danehy said.

Madison did a double take. She thought she must have heard her teacher wrong. He never understood, especially when it came to lateness.

"Finally, there will be no more pop quizzes for the remainder of the year," Mr. Danehy said, looking around. No one knew how to respond.

Of course, there was a catch. Just seconds later, Mr. Danehy let out a rough little laugh. "Just kidding!" he crooned. "A little springtime humor for my favorite students!"

The class sat in silence, semistunned by their teacher's prank.

Of course, Madison should have known better. There was no way Mr. Danehy would give up on his crusade against students' being late, his mission to conquer the textbook reading assignment, or his best booby-trap device of all: the pop quiz.

"I . . . can't . . . believe . . . it. . . ." Ivy flipped her red hair and sighed. "I thought he was *serious*," she whined. "How can he possibly play a joke on us like that? That is just so . . . so . . . unfair."

"Now that everyone's awake," Mr. Danehy continued, "let's get to the heart of the matter: our latest assignment. Well, it's more of a project, really."

"Another project?" Chet Waters cried from across the science room. Chet was the twin brother of Madison's BFF Fiona, and he always had something to say.

"Problem, Mr. Waters?" Mr. Danehy replied. "How can you object when you don't even know what the project is yet?"

Chet gulped. "Oh, yeah," he said. "I just figured, since the year was almost over, that maybe . . ."

"*Almost* is the key word in your sentence," Mr.

Danehy said. "*Almost*. Not yet. Not now. We still have a few good work weeks left in us. Don't we, students?"

Half of the class nodded in silent agreement. The other half stared down at their notebooks, wondering how they could possibly face *another* science project. It felt as if they'd done about ten of them already that year.

But Madison knew that the boom had not even been lowered yet. She knew that the worst news about this latest science project was still to come.

She was right.

"One more thing," Mr. Danehy went on. "Many of you have requested an alternate science partner. But I have decided that you will be doing these end-of-year projects with your usual science partners. It gives you one last chance to prove your mettle. Show me your best teamwork."

Madison groaned. It looked like she'd be working with Ivy . . . again.

"What's *mettle*?" someone asked from a seat near Madison.

"Dumbo," Ivy muttered under her breath. "Who doesn't know what 'metal' means? Silver, gold—*duh*!"

"I think Mr. Danehy means another kind of mettle," Madison piped up. "It's a different word."

"Whatever you say, Miss Brainiac," Ivy said. "Why do you always have to be such a show-off?"

Madison rolled her eyes. Class had only just begun, and she and Ivy had already been at each other's throats for several minutes: first in the hallway and now here.

Mr. Danehy handed out a stack of papers and circled the room. On the top page, Madison saw a boldfaced list of science-project topics, covering a range of subjects that had been discussed throughout seventh grade.

"I can't believe he really expects us to write a paper on this stuff. . . ." Ivy said.

"And do experiments. . . ." Madison added. "Don't forget."

"How can I forget? He's completely unfair and unrealistic and. . . ."

Ivy would have kept listing negatives for hours. Madison was sure of that.

But Mr. Danehy noticed Ivy's grumbling.

"Excuse me, Ms. Daly . . ." he called out from the front of the classroom. "Is there something you would like to share with the rest of us?"

Although science class had been torturous all year, there had been high points, and this was sure to be another one. This was one of the moments when Mr. Danehy saw right through Ivy's facade and called attention to her shenanigans in class. Madison was gladder than glad that despite her science teacher's many, *many* flaws and annoying little habits, like telling nonjokes that he thought were just hysterical, he still managed to see through the enemy as if she were made of plastic wrap.

"I don't care what he says," Ivy muttered to Madison when Mr. Danehy finished embarrassing her.

"You wouldn't," Madison mumbled. She turned back to the page of instructions in front of her and began reading through them.

> Solve a problem using the scientific method. State your problem, do research, make an educated guess about your problem, and then prove your hypothesis is correct. Describe what you do. Then, create a display to show your results. Use pie charts and graphs if you need to. Pictures and detailed notes are good, too.

The suggested list of project ideas looked complicated. Madison wasn't sure about *any* of the choices. How could she and her partner—especially *this* partner—possibly narrow it down?

- What would happen to weather if the earth were a cube?
- How does mouthwash work as a germ-killer?
- Why is the sky blue?
- How do you make salt water potable?
- Does your eye color affect your vision?
- Can you make frogs jump with static electricity?
- Is there a link between the movement of the Earth and the damage caused by a tsunami?
- On which food does fungus grow best?
- Can you make six different kinds of slime and determine the slimiest?

Madison's eyes locked on to the slime idea. That was *perfect* for Poison Ivy, wasn't it? This enemy was the slimiest of them all.

Unfortunately, slime or no slime, Ivy wouldn't even talk about the project, opting instead to examine her cell phone and pick at some pale polish on her fingernails.

"I'm so revolting," Ivy said after a while.

"Huh?" Madison's eyes widened. *You said it, not me,* she thought. *And yes, you certainly are revolting.* Of course, Madison knew Ivy had just gotten the words mixed up—again.

"You mean you want to stage a revolt?" Madison asked, clarifying and trying very hard not to laugh too loud at Ivy's linguistic mistake.

"Yes, *revolt*, that's what I said," Ivy barked.

"I understand that you're upset, but we can't revolt, Ivy. We have to get this project done," Madison said. "It's the last one of the year. We can do this if we work together."

Madison sounded like a cheerleader.

"Get real, Madison. No one cares about this dumb project," Ivy replied. She pursed her lips and spit out each word as if it pained her to even say it. "Mr. Danehy can fail us if he wants."

Madison's eyes widened again. She wanted to blurt out some kind of nasty retort or shout, "Well, I care!" but she said nothing. Right now her brain hurt from arguing. She'd have to find the right words, not necessarily the quickest ones.

When the class bell rang for lunch, Madison scooted out of her lab seat. Hart met her over by the door, and they left and walked to the cafeteria together.

"So, you and Poison Ivy are partners again?" Hart teased. "Party time."

"Funny," Madison said.

"Not as funny as Mr. Danehy's joke at the start of class, though, right?"

"Right," Madison smiled. "Here's my problem: Ivy won't do the project."

"She has to do it," Hart said. "She'll fail if she doesn't."

"Ivy says she doesn't care," Madison said.

"What a liar," Hart said. "You know Ivy. She always has to be the big shot. She cares—big-time."

"And she says *I'm* the one who needs all the attention," Madison said.

"Well, that's true. . . ." Hart smiled.

Madison punched him in the arm. They laughed their way down the hall.

Once they reached the cafeteria, Hart wandered off to meet up with the rest of the guys: Dan, Egg, Chet, and Drew. Madison looked for her girlfriends and found four of them clustered together around the salad bar: Aimee, Fiona, Lindsay, and Madhur. Thankfully, Ivy was nowhere in sight.

The five friends got their food and went to sit at their usual orange table in the back of the lunchroom. Madison picked at the food on her tray, but she seemed to have lost her appetite. She'd ordered a plate with steamed vegetables and lasagna, but it jiggled a little too much. Aimee didn't seem to mind. She picked at Madison's broccoli, popping little florets into her mouth one by one.

"So, my family decided what we're doing this summer, and it is just amazing," Madhur announced to everyone. Her eyes grew bright. "We're going to Pakistan and India!"

"Wow," Madison said. "You're visiting Punjab?"

"You bet," Madhur said. "My family's homeland."

"My brother will be so bummed out," Fiona blurted. "I know he was hoping to see more of you this summer."

"Really?" Madhur asked innocently.

Madison, Aimee, Fiona, and Lindsay all shot Madhur one of those "Oh, come on!" looks.

Madhur grinned. "I swear, Chet does not like me like that," she insisted.

"Yeah, right," Fiona said, glancing toward the other end of the table, where the boys were sitting. They couldn't hear the girls' conversation, thankfully.

"Anyway," Madhur said, changing the subject, "my mother told me about the trip, and I almost flipped. Grandmamma is going, too. They took me one other time when I was three or whatever, but I don't remember much of that trip. This will be different. This will be so real."

"Pakistan and India are so far away," Madison mused.

Madhur grinned. "I wish I could bring all of you there with me. Now, *that* would be a blast."

"My family might go to California again this summer," Fiona said, "but that's not as exciting as a trip halfway across the globe. And our trip is really just for my dad. I think he may be interviewing for a new job again. He keeps talking about how much he misses the West Coast."

Madison didn't know what to say to that. Lately, she'd been more and more worried that Fiona's family might move back to their old state and leave Far Hills permanently.

"Aren't you going to England again with your aunt Mimi?" Aimee asked Lindsay.

Lindsay nodded. "Dad's going, too. I think he's renting a flat for a month, in London or somewhere in the country. I can't remember. We'll be riding horses, though. I love that."

"Wow, horses? And a whole *month*?" Madison asked, her voice tinged with mild envy. She had never been to London.

"You guys may be massive jet-setters, but *I'm* going somewhere cooler than all of you this summer," Aimee chimed in.

"You are?" Madison asked, bewildered. "Where?"

"Far Hills. Have you heard of it? It's this totally unhip place. Ha-ha-ha . . ."

Aimee was fake-laughing, but everyone else was laughing for real.

"Seriously," Aimee continued, "I'm stuck here for the summer, but it's all good, because Mom is letting me take this advanced dance class. I'm going to learn more tap and jazz from this famous teacher who has a course in New York City. Maybe I'll get more dance solos next year. . . ."

"You're all so busy," Madison said. "I guess I'll hang out at the town pool. La-la-la . . . all alone . . ."

"Aw, Maddie . . ." Aimee said, reaching over to squeeze Madison's shoulder. "Stop exaggerating. That isn't how it's going to be, and you know it."

"Summer after seventh grade, and everyone gets to fly around the world and take exciting classes—except for me," Madison grumbled.

"We won't all be gone at the same time, Maddie," Lindsay said, "and you won't be alone. We're always with you."

"With my luck," Madison said, "I'll end up with Ivy Daly as my pool partner this summer. Now, wouldn't that be perfection?"

Everyone laughed again—louder this time.

"Hey! What's so funny?" Hart asked from the other end of the table.

The boys shoved closer. Hart squeezed in next to Madison; Dan moved near Lindsay; Chet cozied up to

Madhur; and Egg and Fiona squished in together. Aimee was the only one who was without a crush at the table. Drew was a friend, nothing more. She had her eye on another seventh grader, Ben Buckley, anyway; and nothing could change her mind about that crush, even if it was never going to be realized. Madison thought about how funny it was that the five of them had started the year solo but had all ended up either paired with or liking some boy. They each would head into eighth grade with real boyfriends, unless, of course, everything fell apart over the summer.

"Which one of you guys is going to be in Far Hills this summer?" Madison asked the table.

"As far as I know, I'm lifeguarding again at the Far Hills pool," Hart said. "Unless something changes . . ."

"I'm a fool for the pool," Egg said.

"I'm working in one of my dad's offices downtown," Drew said. "I have my own cubicle."

"I'm at the animal clinic all summer," Dan groaned, "but you guys knew that already."

Madison chuckled to herself. Was it possible that her post-seventh-grade summer might be spent more with boys than with girls? She wondered if that was good, or weird, or both.

Eventually, the boys got distracted and drifted back to their side of the table.

"Listen. No matter what happens this summer,"

Madison whispered, "we have to stick together, right? Like those girls in *The Sisterhood of the Traveling Pants*."

"Maybe we should get our own pants," Lindsay joked. "If they were magic, even I would fit into them, right?"

Madison smiled. Lindsay was always stressing out about her weight. So was Aimee, for that matter, but for opposite reasons. It didn't seem to matter whether someone was chubby or skinny—nobody ever felt just right. The only person Madison knew who didn't care so much about her body was Fiona. She ate whatever she wanted, exercised, and hardly ever freaked out about her wardrobe.

"Come on! We don't need a pair of pants to keep us together!" Aimee said.

"But no matter what," Madison started to say again, "we will stay in touch, right?" She needed confirmation from everyone in the group.

"Forever and ever," Aimee chirped.

"Till the end of summer . . ." Lindsay said.

"Till the ends of the earth!" Madhur added.

"Thanks," Madison said, even though she wondered if anyone could really stay friends for *that* long. "I feel much better."

"Of course, first we have to get through the last weeks of school," Fiona reminded everyone.

And the last weeks of Poison Ivy, Madison added silently.

Chapter 3

"What are you doing out here?" Mom asked Madison. "Is your dad coming over soon?"

"Yeah, I figured I'd wait outside for him and Stephanie. It's still so warm out," Madison replied.

"Writing in your files?" Mom asked.

Madison nodded. "How did you know?"

"Moms know everything."

Rowooorrrooooooo!

Phinnie howled and chased Mom's ankles down the porch steps. The air was sticky and hot for his late-day walk.

"Dad's late. As usual," Madison said.

Mom let Phin roam around the front yard, sniffing at flowers and bushes. He didn't have on his leash, but no one worried. Phin never wandered very far. This was one dog that didn't get all worked up about other dogs or cats in the neighborhood. The only thing that could possibly send him racing across the street might be a rabbit or a possum, or maybe even a skunk. But there weren't too many of those around.

"How's the last month of school shaping up?" Mom asked, taking a seat on a wicker chair next to Madison's.

"Busy," Madison replied.

"Busy with what? Tell me."

"Mr. Danehy gave us this ultracomplicated, super hard project to finish, and I'm stuck with Ivy as a partner *again*," Madison whined.

"That's too bad," Mom said.

She knew the score when it came to Madison and Ivy. Madison had told her all the details of Ivy's copying and her cheating throughout the school year.

"I still remember when you and Ivy were close," Mom said, shaking her head. "When did she become such a troublemaker?"

"She's not all I have to worry about," Madison confided. "We're also having this musical revue at school, and I have to participate. I have to *sing*!"

"Why don't you do something behind the scenes, like you did for the school play?" Mom suggested.

Madison's eyes opened wide. Inside her head

there was a click, as if a switch had been turned on and a lightbulb had been lit.

"Fantastic idea, Mom!" Madison cried, instantly energized. "I don't have to go onstage, do I? Why didn't I think of that?"

She breathed a deep sigh of relief. Mom leaned over and put her hands on Madison's knees.

"Maddie . . . honey bear . . ." Mom said, "there's something I need to tell you."

Madison looked right into Mom's eyes. "Tell me," she said, feeling a flip-flopping inside her belly. "What?"

"As you know, I've been working a lot," Mom said, "and I got that big promotion at Budge Films. . . ."

Madison nodded. "Uh-huh." What was Mom hinting at?

"Well, there's another executive film producer job coming up . . . at another company . . . a bigger company."

"Uh-huh." Madison felt as if she were on the edge of her seat. Was Mom about to tell her that they would be packing up and moving to the Yukon, or the Amazon, or somewhere else completely remote?

"So, we're moving?"

"Not exactly," Mom said. "My *job* may be moving . . ."

"So . . . either way . . . my world is about to implode!" Madison said very dramatically.

"Don't say that," Mom said. "I'm not doing anything *yet*."

"Fiona's dad is thinking about changing his job, too," Madison said. "There must be something in the air."

"That's funny," Mom said. "Mrs. Waters didn't mention anything to me."

"If you get this new, more important job, does it mean I'll see *less* or *more* of you?" Madison asked.

Mom shook her head. "I just don't know yet."

"Okay. I won't stress until you know for sure," Madison said.

Mom clapped her hands, summoning Phin back up on to the porch. He had a fat black stick between his teeth, which she promptly removed.

"Let's talk more later," Mom said.

"Sure," Madison said, even though she felt decidedly *unsure*.

As soon as Mom took Phin inside the house again, Madison turned back to her laptop to open a new file.

 Big Changes

```
So here's what I know:
All my BFFs are traveling for the
summer. And I'm not. I'm in a science
nightmare with Poison Ivy. The musical revue
is coming at me like a speeding train.
And now Mom is leaving Budge to be
```

some big shot at another film company?

Rude Awakening: Just when I think I have it all figured out, "it" takes off like a rocket, leaving me *way* in the dust.

Okay, I'm not in the dust exactly. Just this afternoon, Aimee suggested that I sign up for one of her summer dance classes so I wouldn't feel too out of touch and so I could limber up, not that I'm in major need of limbering. Or maybe I am? If I'm going to survive all these changes, I definitely need to get more flexible.

On top of everything else that's going on in school and life, we got word 2day that the teachers organized this last-minute field trip (a "reward," they called it, HA!) to Lake Dora. It's just a day trip for the seventh grade, but I guess it IS something to look forward to. I don't know anymore. All these things blur together. I can't forget to have Mom sign the permission slip before next week.

Madison hit SAVE, because it was getting late and she still needed to check her e-mail. The little mailbox icon blinked. That meant, "Come and get it!"

She clicked on the icon, and a larger-than-expected e-mail list appeared.

FROM	SUBJECT
✉ GoGramma	My Itinerary
✉ GoGramma	My Itinerary

☒ GoGramma	My Itinerary
☒ Angelina77	Re: My Itinerary
☒ DR_BigBOB	Re: My Itinerary
☒ Sk8ingboy	Txt trub
☒ Dantheman	Animal Clinic Summer
☒ Bigwheels	W^

Madison scrolled through the different e-mails. Naturally, Gramma Helen had hit the SEND button a few times too many.

From: GoGramma
To: MadFinn (Maddie), Angelina77
(Angie), DR_BigBOB (Bob),
FF_Budgefilms (Fran)
Subject: My Itinerary
Date: Thurs 8 Jun 11:01 AM
_____
How wonderful to know that I will
be seeing all of you in Far Hills
in just a few weeks. I think having
Maddie's moving-up ceremony as an
excuse to get family together was
just perfect. Thanks, Maddie.

I will be flying into LaGuardia
Airport this time, direct from
O'Hare in Chicago on Monday, June
19--a few days early. Fran and I
discussed, so no one has to worry
about getting me there, ok? If
there's any problem, let me know.

Oh, and dears--I plan on making a
big feast, so everyone come ready
to eat. Angie and Bob--don't forget
to bring photos of your beautiful
garden. You promised.

All my love

Gramma Helen

After Gramma Helen's e-mail, there were two
responses: one from Madison's aunt Angie and
another from her uncle Bob, Mom's brother. Both
were checking in to see if Mom needed any help
with the party.

The family get-together to celebrate Moving Up
Day was really, as Gramma Helen said, a great excuse
to get the family together in the warm weather. Ever
since the Big D, Madison's extended family had not
had much face time together. And it wasn't just
Mom's side of the family that was coming. Dad's
brother, Rick, and his wife, Violet, were coming from
Canada. And of course, Madison's stepmother,
Stephanie, was coming.

So, although the day of moving up to eighth
grade wasn't necessarily a major event (not as big as
a high school or college graduation), for the Finns
and the Hirsches it would be a major bash. Madison
just hoped it wouldn't make her want to *bash* her
head into a wall. After all, as she knew only too well,

sometimes mothers and fathers and exes and aunts and uncles just couldn't mix.

After the e-mails about the family get-together and Gramma Helen's planned arrival date, Madison checked the other e-mails in her box, from three of her favorite people. The first was from Hart.

From: Sk8ingboy
To: MadFinn
Subject: Txt trub
Date: Thurs 8 Jun 3:51 PM
Hey im trying to txt u right now but I can't. I think my dad had the service suspended fm my cell. DTS?! I guess last month he got the bill and there were like a billion messages I sent that cost all this xtra $$ so he got real mad. He sez I have 2 pay him back or ditch the phone. N e way, that means we have txt trub, b/c I can't get txting fm u either. 9ML8R?

Madison smiled. She liked the idea that Hart was upset about not being able to get in touch. That meant he cared, didn't it?

Sigh.

After Hart's message, Madison read through a quick note from Dan. He had sent information about summer volunteer schedules at the animal clinic.

Madison realized that clinic volunteer work was probably a great option for her, in addition to all the other things she had planned. Madison hit REPLY and told Dan that she'd check with her mom and plan her own summer clinic schedule.

Of course, Madison saved the best message for last. Bigwheels was checking in from Washington. She'd been writing a lot lately.

```
From: Bigwheels
To: MadFinn
Subject: W^
Date: Thurs 8 Jun 4:19 PM
```
LTNE-M! HAY? IMU! Wouldn't it be funny 2 write ONLY in abbreviations? I tried that yesterday w/another online friend fm school and I got soooo messed up. But seriously--HAY --HOW ARE YOU? We're practically 8th graders now & I am soooo psyched. Have we really been keypals for a whole YEAR???

Is yr mom having that big party u told me about? +:>) Well . . . I told my mom about what u said and she decided to steal the idea so now we're having EVERYONE--my uncles, cousins, aunts, grandmas, and everyone else--over for BBQ.

U were right about tests--we have a
bunch this week and next week 2. I
thought we would be done 4 the yr
but NSL. Boo-hoo. I am afraid I
might fail math although my mom got
me a tutor just in case. She wants
me 2 apply to this ritzy private
school. Help!

BTW: Did I tell u my parents were
THIS CLOSE to making a reservation
to fly to NEW YORK CITY??? Dad's
cousin lives there. But now the
plans have been nixed. :>(

BTW 2: Reggie asked me to the
junior high dance 4 the end of the
yr. Do u have a dance 2?

OK. I better go now. SUS! Well,
that should be W2US!

Yours till the sun beams,

Bigwheels aka Vicki

P.S.: WBSTS

Madison smiled. This was one of those messages
that made her feel virtually hugged. Bigwheels was
an expert at that.

Madison had just begun typing her response when she heard the sound of a motor from out in front of the house. A moment later, a car turned in to the driveway. Madison glanced up to see Dad behind the wheel. Stephanie was next to him in the front seat. Smiling, Madison waved.

"Hello-o-o-o-o-o!" Stephanie waved back from the rolled-down window.

"Hey," Madison called. She snapped the laptop lid shut. "Just a sec!"

She ran into the hall, where Mom was standing. They embraced and said their good-byes.

"I'll see you when your dad brings you back," Mom said sweetly.

Madison nodded. Phin nuzzled the backs of her knees, and it tickled.

"See you, too, my little Phinster," Madison joked around. She bent down to scratch Phin's ears. "Seriously, Phinnie, be a good boy for Mom."

Dad lightly honked the horn. "Let's boogie!" he called out.

Mom stood in the doorway and waved good-bye to everyone, including Stephanie. Over the course of seventh grade, Madison had noticed that Mom and Stepmom had actually become a lot friendlier. Despite the Big D, it seemed that the last year had brought everyone a little closer together—almost like one big, happy family with a few blocks, or miles, in between.

Then again, as Mr. Danehy had said in class, *almost* was the operative word.

When it came to families, just about anything *could* happen.

And when it came to Madison's family, anything *would* happen.

Madison just had to wait a few weeks to see how everything played itself out.

Chapter 4

Outside the locked choral room, Aimee twirled impatiently, and then twirled some more. Madison watched as her BFF tried to do three complete rotations without losing her balance. Of course, she could. As far as Madison was concerned, when it came to dance, Aimee could do anything.

"You're making me dizzy," Fiona groaned, grabbing Aimee by the sleeve. "You have to stop."

"I can't stop," Aimee teased, spinning around again. "Wheee-hooo!"

Madison giggled. "Yes, you can stop," she declared, reaching out for Aimee's sleeve. "Aim . . ."

Aimee finally stopped the spin. She threw her arms up and quickly leaned into the wall to keep from falling flat, even though spins like that rarely made a ballerina dizzy.

Madison and her two BFFs slid down to the floor and sat cross-legged, still waiting for the choral room to open up so the first official revue meeting could begin. A teacher was supposed to open the door, but so far only a crowd of students had shown up.

"Guess what?" Aimee whispered to Madison and Fiona. "Ben might try out."

Aimee's eyes lit up when she said the name of her crush.

"*Your* Ben—is going to sing and dance?" Fiona asked in disbelief. "Aim, you're making that up."

"I am not," Aimee said defensively. "He said . . ."

"He said it to be nice," Fiona said.

"Aim," Madison made a face. "Ben is, like, one of the shyest guys in school. How could he possibly do the revue?"

Aimee got a worried look on her face, and Madison realized that she'd just popped her best friend's bubble.

"He probably just said it because he likes you— and he wants you to keep liking him . . . or something like that . . ." Madison said, trying to make Aimee feel better.

"Chet told me Ben was chosen to do the big speech for our class on Moving Up Day," Fiona said. "He's probably focused on that."

"Ben is our class valedictorian?" Madison asked. "Since when?"

"He's the obvious choice," Aimee said, smiling wide. "He's the smartest kid in our class, don't you think?"

"Yeah, he's a super-duper-califragilisticexpialido-cious genius," Madison said, borrowing the funny word from the *Mary Poppins* song.

Just then, the choral room door made a loud clicking sound. The choral directors, Mr. and Mrs. Montefiore, opened the double doors wide. The two of them were both dressed in navy blue and white. Mr. Montefiore had on one of his ugly blue-striped ties over a wrinkled white shirt. Mrs. Montefiore wore a dark blue dress with thin white stripes. Being a matched set fashionwise wasn't the only way that they seemed the same. This couple talked alike, walked alike, and even laughed the same way.

The kids rushed inside. Madison, Aimee, and Fiona staggered toward three seats near the middle of the room. When everyone finally settled in, the room was packed.

"Is Egg doing the revue, or what?" Madison asked Fiona, who always knew where Egg was—and where he was headed.

"No," Fiona shook her head. "He said he's too busy with the school Web site. Of course, I told him that was a lame-o excuse. Don't you think?"

Madison and Aimee nodded.

Mrs. Montefiore tapped her baton on the music stand at the front of the room.

"Welcome, students!" she declared in her singsong voice. "Mr. M. and I are beyond thrilled about this year's revue. To see so many seats filled with students ready to entertain us . . . Well, it brings genuine tears to my eyes. . . ."

"Who is she kidding?" Aimee moaned under her breath. "Those cannot be real tears."

Fiona and Madison stifled a giggle.

Mrs. Montefiore asked everyone to stand up and do a few stretches. No matter what kind of rehearsal it was or what time of day it was, she always added in some kind of acrobatic element. One time, Mrs. Montefiore had had everyone in the room act "like the wind" and blow themselves around the room. It was fun for about thirty seconds—until two kids collided and one got the *real* wind knocked out of him.

Madison glanced around the room to see who else she recognized. There were surprisingly few seventh graders, a whole bunch of eighth graders, and a cluster of ninth graders sitting together in the front of the room. Although Egg was indeed *not* there that day, Madison saw his sister, Mariah, and waved at her to come over.

Mariah Diaz was a wild ninth grader; today she had her hair streaked pink, a color that was most definitely not allowed in the school dress code.

Madison guessed that Mariah had only just put the color in the day before. She was always taking risks like that.

"Hey, Maddie," Mariah said when she came over to Madison and the others. No matter what, Mariah always made the time to say hello and be friendly. In many ways, she was the exact opposite of her annoying sibling.

"Hey, Mariah," Madison responded. "Are you in the revue?"

Mariah nodded. "Backstage, I think. I'm helping with the whole set and backdrops, working with the art department. Of course, I won't be doing much more than painting. You know the deal: teachers are in charge. But I get to do a few of my own designs, which is cool."

"Wow," Madison said, impressed.

Mariah nodded. "My mom wanted me to play a piano solo, too. I don't know if I want to perform though, unless it means getting Egg out here to play his head like a coconut!"

Madison giggled. "Are you excited about graduating?"

"Sure," Mariah said. "*If* I graduate. Today, Principal Bernard said that if I showed up again with another inappropriate hair color, he'd suspend me."

"He wouldn't do that!" Madison cried.

Mariah nodded. "It's nothing compared to what my mom will do to me. When she saw the pink this morning, she threatened to shave my head."

"I think it looks kind of cool," Madison said.

"Face it," Fiona piped up, "you *always* look cool, Mariah."

Mariah smiled modestly. "Thanks. You do, too."

"Too bad no cool rubbed off on your brother," Aimee joked.

Mariah laughed hard. "Hey, I better sit down. Mr. M. is giving me the evil eye. Plus, his toupee is about to fall off. Check it out."

Madison and the others shot a look at the music teacher just in time to catch him readjusting his hairpiece.

As the meeting continued, Mr. Montefiore explained how the entire group of participants would choose from a list of musical numbers, mostly Broadway tunes. Most people who volunteered to sing and dance would be singing group numbers, while a select few would do their whole act solo or in pairs. Mr. and Mrs. Montefiore sat down at the piano and belted out a few examples of the songs they'd be singing from shows like *Guys and Dolls*, *Pippin*, and *Bye Bye Birdie*.

Madison thought about what Ivy had said to her in the hallway, about how Madison wasn't "exactly" a performer and how she "practically" fell apart when she got onstage. Unfortunately, Madison had to admit that her enemy was right on target. Despite minor successes in speaking onstage at the Junior

World Leaders Conference or presenting papers in front of an entire class, Madison Francesca Finn was way better *behind* the scenes.

"Okay. I just decided. I'm absolutely not singing," Madison declared to her friends.

"Maddie," Aimee said, "If you're singing in a group, no one will hear you—"

"*I'll* hear me," Madison said.

"You're too hard on yourself, Maddie," Fiona said.

"I'm just realistic," Madison said.

"Well, I'm singing!" Fiona chirped. "And I know Lindsay wants to sing, too. Maybe she and I can do a duet. I'll ask Mrs. Montefiore."

"What's Madhur doing?" Aimee asked.

Madison and Fiona both shrugged. No one knew for sure.

After a chaotic hour of song selecting, the large group was dismissed. Madison saw Ivy skip out of the room as if she didn't have a care in the world. A few rows beyond her, Mariah exited the hall, too, her pink-haired head held high. Despite her outsider stance, Madison looked up to Mariah a lot. Egg didn't realize how lucky he was to have her for a big sister.

"We'll post the final list of participants up on the main bulletin board in the lobby by tomorrow at lunch, along with a complete schedule of run-throughs and practice times," Mr. Montefiore said as everyone left the room.

"Thank you, dears, for coming!" Mrs. Montefiore gushed.

Madison had made plans to walk home together with Aimee and Fiona, but on the way out of the choral room, she remembered that she'd left a notebook in Mr. Danehy's classroom. The purple notebook was important, because it contained her preliminary project notes. That night, Madison planned on surfing the Internet for more facts and figures related to the list of topics.

As Madison walked toward the science room, she saw that there weren't too many students—in fact, there weren't too many people at all—left in the building, although Madison narrowly missed a collision with a custodian and his very large bucket of dirty mop water.

Luckily, Mr. Danehy's door was ajar, which meant that he was probably still inside. He never left his classroom open at night. There were Bunsen burners, glass jars containing lab specimens, and a whole host of other valuable items stored inside. He knew that pranksters could very easily enter his room and cause mayhem if he didn't lock it up when he left.

"Mr. Danehy?" Madison said as she pushed the door open.

Her teacher was not alone.

"Oh, I was just talking about you," Ivy blurted out as soon as she saw Madison come through the door.

"What are you doing here?" Madison asked. Ivy wasn't the type to stay after school unless she absolutely had to.

"The question is," Ivy said in her most saccharine voice, "what are *you* doing here?"

"Ms. Finn," Mr. Danehy said, "Ms. Daly informs me that the two of you have not yet chosen a topic for the project."

"No? Well . . ." Madison was completely taken aback.

Ivy held up a notebook. It was purple.

Madison's notebook!

"I was just showing Mr. Danehy our class notes," Ivy said, holding it up.

"*Our* class notes? Wait—that's—wait—" Madison tried to speak fast, but it came out all garbled. She was too surprised to get the words right.

"Girls, girls, girls," Mr. Danehy said, holding up his hands like a referee. "I understand your concerns, but remember: the notes are irrelevant. Our work habits are not negotiable."

Madison must have been making a "Huh?" face because Mr. Danehy continued with his explanation. His words quickly got a lot clearer.

"Ms. Finn," Mr. Danehy said, "I need you and Ms. Daly to work *together*. You *do* know what that word means, don't you?"

"Yes, of course—"

"Because I don't like what I'm seeing. It appears

Ivy here has been working much harder on the project notes."

Madison started to reply. "But I was working—"

"We'll figure it out," Ivy added in her best Pollyanna voice.

"I guess . . ." Madison said.

"No guesswork involved," Mr. Danehy said. "Either you will or you won't, Ms. Finn. I know you'll do the right thing."

Madison bubbled up inside, like a pot ready to boil over.

"Very well," Mr. Danehy said, rubbing his palms together. "Are you satisfied now, Ms. Daly? I assume there will be no further conflict here. Correct? After all, you do have one of the best students as your partner."

After all of that conflict and defense of *Ivy*, Madison was further taken aback by Mr. Danehy's backhanded compliment. At least he wasn't totally taking sides.

No sooner had Mr. Danehy ushered the two girls out of the classroom than Madison and the enemy turned to face each other like wild animals. Ivy thrust the purple notebook right at Madison's mid-section.

"Here!" Ivy spat. "Here's your dumb notebook. Better hang on to it, huh?"

"You're so . . . so . . . pathetic," Madison cried, finally—*finally!*—finding the right words. "I can't believe you would go to Mr. Danehy and pretend that you worked on *any* of these notes. I can't believe how low you can sink. . . ."

"*Glug, glug, glug,*" Ivy taunted, as if she were pretending to sink in reality. Then she rolled her eyes and walked away. "See you later—*much*," Ivy said, waving her hand without once looking back at Madison's face.

Madison pushed the notebook into her orange bag and headed for the school lobby. If she ran fast enough, maybe she could catch up with her BFFs. Or at least she could catch Aimee at home. She needed a real friend to shake off these bad feelings. After a long walk with Phin, Aimee, and Aimee's dog, Blossom, Madison knew she would feel better.

After all, anything was better than dealing with Poison Ivy.

Chapter 5

 Mad Science

Poison Ivy is the bane of my existence, the thorn in my side, AND the pain in my neck. Wow, I sound like my Gramma Helen, who's always coming up with those kooky sayings. Kidding aside though, today was DEFINITELY the next-to-the-last straw with Ivy.

Since Ivy doesn't really care about this project and since she thinks LYING and passing off my work as hers is acceptable, then I can just pick whatever topic I want and DO whatever I want. So far I think I am partial to the "Why Is the Sky Blue?"

question for a lot of reasons. I like blue, sunny skies more than I like rainy ones or dark ones. Plus, Dad gave me this prism charm once that refracts light and makes rainbows on my wall. I'd like to know more about how all that light stuff works.

So: no report on the earth as a cube (too hard), no basic chemistry (too impossible), and definitely no fungus (too gross). I'll aim higher than all that. The blue sky really is the limit.

Rude Awakening: With a plan to show Ivy up, I give new meaning to the words "mad scientist." Better make sure that I keep any rants confined to my files--just in case. :>)

Madison reread her file and pressed SAVE.

Sure, she'd been mad at Ivy plenty of times over the years, but she'd never steamed like this. The camel's back really was broken. It was time to get back at the enemy for all those cruel digs, the ongoing flirtation with Hart, the nasty disposition, the mega-annoying pink cell phone case, and so much more. Maybe some of the revenge reasons were petty, but the majority weren't—and majority ruled.

It seemed like such a distant memory—the days when Madison and Ivy had called each other friends.

Particular memories from second grade and before leaped into Madison's head like lightning bolts. She remembered the days when the two of them had dressed alike and even talked alike. Their favorite outfits: capri pants in matching colors, T-shirts with cap sleeves and little sayings like "Cutie Pie" or "Honey Bug" printed on them. Their favorite sayings: "Getouttatown" and "No, *you're* the bestest!"

There were a lot of good—no, great—memories.

In first grade, Ivy and Madison had been practically inseparable. They had learned to read together (along with Amelia Bedelia, Madison's favorite misfit). They wrote their own picture books about life on a teddy bear farm (starring Madison's own bear, Beary). Once, they had even started their own mud pie business, hawking pie tins filled with muck all over Ivy's neighborhood. And people had actually bought them.

Back when Madison and Ivy were BFFs, Aimee had been there, too. The three of them would parade around together during school, at recess, and on the weekends, sharing a love of all things Barbie: dolls, clothes, accessories, and, of course, the Super Barbie Camper. No one had had a dog back then, but Ivy had had a cat named Paprika, with red-speckled fur and no claws.

Paprika was the trio's mascot; they treated him as their collective pet. Ivy's dad built a grand tree house in her backyard, and the three friends would drag the cat up there for by-invitation-only Barbie tea parties. Paprika hated it when they decorated his long fur with pink glitter. But Madison, Aimee, and Ivy loved those kitty makeovers.

It was third grade when Joan Kenyon and Roseanne Snyder (aka Phony Joanie and Rose Thorn) came to Far Hills elementary school. That was when things—including the balance of power—began to shift. The two new girls turned Madison's threesome into a fivesome for most of their activities, including the tea parties. In retrospect, Madison should have seen the writing on the wall—and the collapse of the friendship. Ivy started to get more secretive and didn't *always* want to hang out. She even defended Roseanne or Joan when the new girls said not-nice things.

It was a sign of things to come. A *billboard*, actually. From third grade on, it always seemed as though Ivy had something to complain about, and she started to blame Madison for all her problems. Then Ivy began spreading nasty rumors about Madison. Things never went back to the way they were.

Not that Mom and Dad (still married back then) helped much. At the time, they had chalked Madison's big fight up to a "passing phase," and Mom had said stuff like, "Look, Maddie, you'll make and change friends a dozen times before middle school even starts. I don't know why you're letting yourself get so worked up about this."

But of course, Madison *had been* worked up. And she was *still* worked up now, years later. It was as if

Mom had said friendship was disposable. Madison hated the idea of that. She wondered why best friendships didn't come with binding contracts and visitation rights and super glue.

Madison clicked her recent file marked MAD SCIENCE open again. She reread the angriest parts and considered erasing them, but didn't. What else was she supposed to do with all those feelings? Madison scrolled down and began to type one more Rude Awakening. It hit the mark.

Rude Awakening #2: Sometimes the worst of friends make the best of enemies, but you find yourself still hanging on.

As she contemplated those words, something wet and warm tickled Madison's left foot. It was a certain dog's pug nose.

"Hey!" Madison cried, twisting to look. There was Phin, with his doggy grin. In a split second, Madison got her thoughts back on track; she focused again on the end-of-year science project.

She brought up the main search screen on bigfishbowl.com and entered the term "blue sky." The initial hit returned a list of sites. There were at least three that talked about weather and blue skies. There were also several featuring such offerings as: an animation studio; a company that made lasers; and a rock band in Idaho (actual full name: Blue Sky Spaz). And there were other sites related to

Madison's scientific question. So she clicked on those Web addresses for facts and figures. Eyeing the home pages of a few sites, Madison selected text she could use and then cut and pasted it (and a few diagrams, too) into her files, to be printed out later.

The surfing and searching lasted for about an hour, and Madison collected lots of good information. She was about to log off when a little icon in the corner of her screen flashed.

An Insta-Message appeared.

```
<Bigwheels>: well hallooooooo U
<MadFinn>: Hey! HAY?
<Bigwheels>: what else? I'm doing
    homework <groan>
<MadFinn>: last month of school 4 U
    2 right?
<Bigwheels>: {:>} doink!
<MadFinn>: I have a NEW science
    project and a history test next
    wk 2 I'm SWAMPED
<Bigwheels>: GW? I just found out
    I'm in the Nat'l Honor Society
<MadFinn>: wow congrats I wonder who
    got that in our class we won't
    know until awards @ end of
    school
<Bigwheels>: I had straight As this
    yr 2
```

<MadFinn>: u never told me that!!! WOWZA!

<Bigwheels>: nah bragging about grades is gross

<MadFinn>: not always!! & not 2 yr keypals! U should tell me this stuff Vicki!!!!

<Bigwheels>: how's the Hart man?

<MadFinn>: hey sneaky DCTS :>)

<Bigwheels>: LOL ok thanks but seriously how is the Hart breaker?

<MadFinn>: cute nice sweet the usual

<Bigwheels>: do u have a 7th grade prom or something

<MadFinn>: :>(nope just a Moving Up Day

<Bigwheels>: bummer if u had a prom u could get kissed again b4 the end of school

<MadFinn>: <**>

<Bigwheels>: well, u DO want Hart 2 kiss u again right? Just like he did @ that jr conference??

<MadFinn>: I guess so maybe I don't know hmmmmmmmm OF COURSE I DO!!!!

<Bigwheels>: :>Pffft

<MadFinn>: how's that new kid U like?

<Bigwheels>: matt is not into me :>(but I don't care he has bad

54

breath n e way so I never want to kiss him Blech besides I told u reggie asked me 2 the dance

<MadFinn>: mom sez I'm too young to kiss boys & I didn't tell her about kissing Hart she would be sad 2 know that I kept that a secret although I almost told her

<Bigwheels>: moms always want 2 be protective

<MadFinn>: I dunno if I'm ready 2 get THAT serious w/Hart right now

<Bigwheels>: OK so what else ^?

<MadFinn>: update: my enemy will now be known as Madame Evil

<Bigwheels>: <yawn> old newz

<MadFinn>: yah but she's really, REALLY bad these dayz

<Bigwheels>: so blow her off

<MadFinn>: how can I do that when we're partners?

<Bigwheels>: if she talks 2 u, pretend u don't hear

<MadFinn>: and then what?

<Bigwheels>: look @ her like ur looking right thru her

<MadFinn>: how do u know all these tricks?

<Bigwheels>: b/c I've been on the other side. I've been the one who got blown off more times than I

want 2 admit. Haven't u?

\<MadFinn\>: Ur right I never thought of it that way

\<Bigwheels\>: u have been complaining about Poison Ivy/The Black Plague (LOL) 4-evah

\<MadFinn\>: 2day I was thinking about when we were close. What would it take 2 make me & Ivy friends again? I wonder. . . .

\<Bigwheels\>: magic potion? genie in a bottle? end of the world?

\<Finn\>: ur so bad!!

\<Bigwheels\>: this yr I got close again 2 someone who had become my enemy it was WAY weird.

\<MadFinn\>: how did it happen???

\<Bigwheels\>: we were on the same debate team and we got into this argument and then all of a sudden we started laughing b/c we were saying the exact same thing but acting like we were the opposition. It WAS pretty funny.

\<MadFinn\>: so now ur friends again?

\<Bigwheels\>: not friends exactly but I don't hate her as much

\<MadFinn\>: there's no hope for me & Ivy

\<Bigwheels\>: come on there's ALWAYS hope :>)

```
<MadFinn>: im so lucky ur my
    keypal--u totally get me--even
    when I'm feeling my crabbiest
<Bigwheels>: It takes 1 crab to
    know 1 crab LOL
<MadFinn>: OMG it's late I better
    go TTFN
<Bigwheels>: E me 18r
```

Madison clicked the power button off, and the screen sizzled to black. Was there such a thing as staying online *too long*? Her brain felt deep-fried from all that chat.

After shutting the laptop with a loud click, petting Phin, and (barely) brushing her teeth, Madison crawled feetfirst under the blankets. By the time Mom came in to say good night, Madison was halfway to dreamland.

Chapter 6

Mr. and Mrs. Montefiore posted the school revue list prominently in the downstairs school lobby as they said they would, just before the second official meeting of the revue committee. Madison and her friends stopped off to check it out. They could barely see in all the chaos. Seventh, eighth, *and* ninth graders bobbed up and down to find their names.

"Wow!" Aimee shrieked when she saw her own name right at the top of the list. "I'm a choreographer's assistant!"

Madison wanted to laugh. Aimee was jumping up and down as if she'd just won a coveted spot on *American Idol*.

"Oh, no," Aimee said a moment later, in a

much softer voice. "I see Rose on the list, too."

"Yeah," Fiona said, "but she doesn't have 'assistant' after her name. That makes you way more important."

"Oh, yeah," Aimee said, giving her friend a high five.

Lindsay scanned the list for her own name and spotted it quickly under PERFORMERS.

"I'm a performer—and look, so is Fiona!" Lindsay cried. "I wonder what that means."

"It means we are stars!" Fiona said.

"Of course, you are," Madison said with a teeny bit of sarcasm.

Fiona caught the dig, but she still smiled. Then, in the middle of everything, she started to sing. Kids elbowed her as they moved closer to the list to find their names, but Fiona kept right on singing. Somehow, she didn't get embarrassed by things that would have sent most kids diving under a rock.

Madison preferred to keep a safe distance from all the hoopla. She hovered at the fringes of the crowd. Was she even *on* the list?

As she stood there, shifting her weight from one foot to the other, Madison saw Poison Ivy and the drones step up to the list. Ivy looked ecstatic; Rose seemed less enthused; Joanie didn't seem to care one way or the other; they were all whispering.

Madison craned her neck and tried to eavesdrop on their little conversation. She was just close enough to hear—yet far enough away to remain unnoticed.

"I refuse to sing with *them*," were Ivy's exact words. She always sounded as if she were plotting something. Madison could only guess what.

"What are you doing?" Aimee said.

Madison nearly jumped out of her skin. "Aim!" she cried. "I didn't know you were standing right there—" She glanced behind Aimee to see if Ivy and the drones were watching, but they weren't.

"Did you see the list? You're a backstage assistant!" Aimee said. "Wait. That's good, right? That's what you wanted, right?"

Madison breathed a huge sigh of relief. "That means I don't have to sing or dance. Of course it's good," she said.

Just then, Madhur raced over.

"Am I too late? I had to meet with the gym teacher, can you believe it? Did you know they blocked off the third-floor stairwell? I could just scream!"

"Come look for your name," Aimee said as she dragged Madhur over to the side. It was there, right next to Aimee's name, under CHOREOGRAPHY.

"Huh? Choreography?" Madhur said, breaking into a giggle. "I told Mr. Montefiore I'd do anything, but I didn't think I'd have to dance. Aimee, did you plan this?"

"You have to dance with me. . . ." Aimee said.

Madison laughed and nudged Madhur. "Looks like Aimee's roped you in, Maddie One," she said, using the familiar nickname she had given to her.

"Well, as you know, I'm always up for new things, Maddie Two!" Madhur said cheerily. She threw her arm around Aimee's shoulder. "So, I guess I will dance. I just hope I don't fall on my face. Not that I haven't done that before. . . ."

The five pals chuckled and skittered over toward the auditorium, where the second meeting was about to take place. On the way in, Madison bumped right into Mariah.

"Yo! Slow it down, mama," Mariah said, jokingly. "The meeting hasn't even started yet."

"Hey," Madison said, standing up tall. She noticed that Mariah's pink streaks were gone.

"What happened to your—?" Madison pointed to Mariah's head.

"By order of the assistant principal. Ditch the pink or sit out the rest of the year," Mariah said morosely. "I didn't have much choice. My mom was so mad."

"I bet she was," Madison said, smirking. Señora Diaz played by the rules. Of course she had to, since she was a teacher at the school.

"Have you seen Egg?" Mariah asked Madison. "I didn't see his name anywhere on the list. . . ."

Madison looked over at Fiona. "What did Egg tell you again? He can't do it because . . ."

61

"He's too busy with his computer. Something like that," Fiona explained. "He hasn't come to any of the meetings. Hardly any of our guy friends have come. It's a bummer."

"It figures," Mariah grumbled. "I'll talk to him. Maybe there's some way I can blackmail him into it. . . ."

Everyone laughed at the thought of that. Once, Mariah had brought in a photo of Egg, naked, lying on a fuzzy blue rug; it was taken when he was a baby. She showed it to Madison and Aimee and a few other girls. Egg was mortified to know that everyone had seen his bare bottom—even if he was only two at the time the picture had been taken.

As they took their seats, the revue meeting began: loud, chaotic, and overwhelming. It got even more so as the time wore on. Kids pushed one another, diving into half-empty rows. For some reason, there were about three times as many kids at meeting number two as there had been at meeting number one. Another five teacher-advisers had joined the crew, helping Mr. and Mrs. Montefiore organize the crowd.

"Finnster!" someone whispered in Madison's ear. Of course, she knew right away who it was.

Hart.

"Hey," Madison said softly as she turned around to see his face. They walked single file into a row of

62

seats where Fiona and the other girls had dumped their stuff. "I was wondering if you'd show up. And I didn't even think to look for your name on the list," she told him in her sweetest voice. "You're performing, right?"

"Nah," Hart replied. "I'm backstage. Just like you."

"Backstage?" Madison asked. "But I thought you wanted to sing or dance or something else in the spotlight. . . ."

"Nah," Hart said again. "I thought we could hang together instead. After all, these are the last few weeks of school, right?"

"Right," Madison said. "Thanks."

The teacher-advisers spent the entire revue meeting dividing the room into different groups by age, category, and act. Madison and Hart ended up together with a bunch of other seventh-grade performers, including Fiona, her brother Chet, Lindsay, and Drew, who had showed up late. All four of them would perform the same songs, two chipper tunes from the musical *Bye Bye Birdie* called "The Telephone Hour" and "A Lot of Livin' to Do."

Chet fidgeted in his seat. "Maybe I should have done something *invisible* instead of this," he said, eyeing the end of the row.

Madison, Lindsay, and Fiona giggled. They knew he'd only signed on for this revue so he could get a little closer to Madhur. But they opted not to tease

Chet publicly for his crush. That would have embarrassed Madhur even more than him.

As Mr. Montefiore played a medley of tunes, including one called "Sit Down, You're Rocking the Boat," from *Guys and Dolls*, Hart leaned close to Madison. He was so close that she could feel his breath on the side of her neck when he talked. Madison thought about what Bigwheels had said last night during their online chat.

Hands . . .

Hart . . .

Kisses . . .

"What are you thinking about?" Hart asked. His words snapped Madison out of her reverie, and she stared dumbly into his dark eyes.

"Uh . . . homework," Madison stammered.

Of course, Madison couldn't tell him the truth.

I was thinking about you, you, YOU.

"Hey, I was wondering . . ." Hart mumbled. "You want to go to the movies with Drew and Elaine this weekend? I think my dad is going to come with us. And maybe Dan, too."

"You mean Dan *and* Lindsay, right?" Madison said, in a soft voice so Lindsay wouldn't hear. Lindsay was sitting a few seats away.

Hart shook his head. "No, I don't think so. Why? Are they hanging out?"

Madison leaned back, surprised. *Of course they're hanging out, you goofball! You know who*

64

the couples are! It's the end of school, and except for Aimee, we've all paired off. Where have you been?

"Dan didn't say anything?" she asked.

Hart was about to answer when Mrs. Montefiore stood up to the microphone on the auditorium stage.

"Okay, everyone. Let's call it a wrap for today. Students, on your way out of the room, please pick up one of the revue rehearsal schedules. In addition to performers and dancers, we'll be having practice sessions and meetings for prop people, lighting people, set designers, and others. This is the last time we'll meet as such a large group—until, of course, the real show. . . ."

Everyone in the room started to applaud.

"One more thing!" Mrs. Montefiore cried. "According to the latest head count, this is our biggest group ever—and we're more excited than ever! So, thank you, one and all."

Everyone clapped a little louder, and then the scramble began: up the aisles, through the doors, into the outside world. It was a mad scene. Pushed from side to side, Madison clung to Hart on the way out, the fingers of both her hands holding on to the back of his polo shirt. It felt nice to be attached to someone like him.

"Are you okay?" Hart asked, shooting her a quick look.

"Mmmm," Madison grinned and pinched the folds of his shirt a little tighter as she held on.

After leaving the school building (and saying good-bye to Hart), Madison headed home with Aimee. For block after block, Aimee talked nonstop. Madison's ears hurt. "The dance numbers are so-o-o complex and sophisticated, and I'm responsible for *three*—yes, *three*—different dances, and that's more than any of the other assistants are responsible for, including the eighth and ninth graders. How amazing, with a capital A, is that?"

Whew.

Madison didn't know what to say when Aimee got her rant on like that. Was it safer just to listen and nod? That was what she did.

After parting ways (finally) with Queen Chatterbox, Madison headed straight for home. Mom was in the kitchen waiting on a report of all the details of the revue meeting.

"So, tell me . . ." Mom asked with a sly grin.

Madison snagged a fistful of salted pretzels and chuckled. "Tell you what?"

Mom paced around the kitchen. "Are you doing a dance solo, or an operatic aria?" she asked.

"Very cute, Mom," Madison said. "No, I asked for behind-the-scenes, props or set work or lighting. Something like that."

"Good for you, honey bear," Mom said, still pacing. "Sounds like a great adventure."

"Oh, speaking of adventures, I keep forgetting to give you something," Madison said. She produced the crumpled permission slip for the field trip to Lake Dora that had been inside her orange bag for half the week. "You need to sign this."

"What's this? A day trip? Lake Dora?" Mom said. She stopped pacing long enough to read it.

Rowowoworrooooo!

Phin bounded into the kitchen, howling loudly. Madison warmly cradled the pug in her arms and kissed his soft little pointy ears.

Mom started to pace again. If she kept it up, she would make a neat groove in the tiled floor.

"Um . . . Mom? Is everything okay?" Madison asked.

Mom nodded. "I have things on my mind."

Then she stopped in her tracks, scribbled her name along the bottom line of the permission slip, and handed it back to Madison.

"Did I do something?" Madison asked.

"You? No-o-o-o," Mom smiled.

"Then what? Is it your job again?" Madison asked.

"Sometimes you read me like a book," Mom said, collapsing into a kitchen chair. "Here's what happened. I got another call from the other film company. They made me a good offer for the new executive job."

"That's good news!" Madison cried. "You wanted that to happen, right?"

67

"Yes. But . . ." Mom's voice trailed off.

Madison raised an eyebrow. "*But?*"

"But . . . *then* . . . this afternoon . . . the CEO of Budge Films came to me with a bonus incentive and an incredible new project. It's a documentary I've wanted to do for years. Some timing, right?"

"So what is this dream documentary about?" Madison asked.

"They want me to do a Japan travelogue, a story about the island volcanoes and hot springs."

"Whoa. That sounds interesting," Madison said, even though she didn't know much about Japan or any other place in Asia—except India, having done several recent Internet searches. She'd tried to learn about Punjab and all the places where Madhur's family had lived. That was it.

"So, when are you going to make a decision on the new job offer?" Madison asked.

"I don't know," Mom answered solemnly. "What do you think I should do?"

"What do *I* think?" Madison asked in reply, laughing halfheartedly. "Why are you asking what I think?"

"Because," Mom said, squeezing Madison's hands a little harder, "I care what you think. And you have a sixth sense about this stuff."

"I do not," Madison said. "Mom, you're being goofy."

"Seriously, Maddie, you're smart about these

things. That's one of the things I love most about you. You trust your instincts."

"I do?" Madison said incredulously. "Since when?"

"Oh, honey bear," Mom went on, "you've grown so much this year. Seventh grade has been a real turning point for you. I can see it."

"It has?" Madison asked.

Mom nodded. "It has." Then she took a long pause. "So, what should I do?"

"Mom, I don't know—"

"Oh, Maddie," Mom sighed. "I know I should be gunning for the big job . . . and I love the work so much. But I so love being able to travel. If I took the executive role, I'd be in an office more—not traveling around the world. And even though I'd go on shorter trips, I'd probably be away from home a lot more often."

"Away *more*? Wait. You never said that part to me before," Madison said. "You told me the opposite would be true. . . ."

"I didn't want you to get all worked up about it, since I didn't know all the details yet. But today I found out that I'd have to fly to Washington at least once a month—and overseas at least once a month—and—"

"*That* would stink," Madison said.

Mom nodded and ran her fingertips over Madison's cheek. "Any time I'm away from you stinks."

"Okay, then I know exactly what you should do," Madison said.

"Yes?" Mom said, smiling.

"You should take the trip to Japan and stay at Budge," Madison said simply. "Because you want to travel—and because I don't want you to be away from me and Phin any more than you already are. There. I said it."

"Then that's what I'll do," Mom said decisively.

"Just like that?" Madison asked.

"Just like that. And you know," Mom said, "if I do take the Japan project, I'll need someone to come on my first scouting trip with me."

Madison's eyes grew wide. "You will?"

"You know who I want to fly with me?"

"Me?" Madison asked.

Mom nodded. "Who else?"

"When?"

"This summer."

"Really?"

"Truly."

"For how long?"

"I don't know. Maybe three weeks."

"Three weeks? Halfway across the world?" Madison squealed. She instantly thought about Madhur's trip to Pakistan and Lindsay's trip to England. After feeling so sorry for herself, Madison was now being asked to go on a trip, too? This was a dream.

"I have to tell Aimee!" Madison cried. "I have to tell everyone."

"Well, remember, I haven't accepted yet . . . and it's not a sure thing *yet*," Mom said, "but go ahead, call Aimee . . . or e-mail her . . . or whatever it is you're doing these days. She's like a member of our family anyway."

"Thanks, Mom," Madison said as she collected her orange bag and raced out of the kitchen. Forget the phone or laptop. Telling Aimee about this required some serious face time. Madison decided she would run down the street to the Gillespie house. She and Aimee could sit on the roof just outside Aimee's bedroom, as they usually did in the summers and on sleepover nights.

Madison grabbed Phin's leash and hooked it to his collar. Then she headed for the porch and for Aimee's house.

This was way too good to be believed.

And way too good *not* to be shared.

Chapter 7

Madison lay in bed, staring at the shiny alarm clock on her night table. Phin had knocked the digital clock radio off the table the week before and it didn't work anymore, so she was making do with a metal windup alarm clock in the shape of a pink pig. Rather than awakening Madison with bells or chimes, this clock oinked.

Phin hated it. As soon as it went off, he dashed madly under the bed.

"You can come out now," Madison whispered to Phin as she leaned over the side of the mattress. "It's just Piggy. No biggie."

Phin poked his snout out from under the

bedspread and sniffed the rug cautiously.

It wasn't Madison's usual get-up-and-go time. She'd set the pig for an hour earlier than usual. With so much to do, Madison figured she would waste less time sleeping and get more done by getting up earlier. Plus, she was supposed to meet Aimee and Fiona to walk to school together.

Getting up early was no hardship. Madison had been having trouble sleeping these last few weeks. Mom had said it was probably just the end-of-school jitters.

"When you have a ton on your mind," Mom had said, "it's hard to stay still, especially under the covers."

Madison jumped out of the bed and walked slowly over to the large, gilded mirror that hung over a dresser. It was an antique, handed down from Gramma Helen's sister Lou. Madison had never known Lou—short for Louisa—although she'd heard stories over the years. Like many pieces and parts of her own family history, the stories came together over time, like pieces of a puzzle. Sometimes Madison had to fish for the details of her ancestry: who resembled whom, where people grew up and traveled, and so much more.

Distressed to see a giant pimple on her face, reflected in the mirror, Madison made a beeline for the hall bathroom. Phin didn't follow; Madison figured he'd fallen back asleep again. Mom was asleep, too. Madison heard her snoring from out in the hall.

With a quick washing of her face, the use of a cotton ball soaked in toner, and a smear of beige cover-up called Zit-B-Gone, the unwelcome blemish was rendered invisible. Madison pulled her hair into a braid and fixed the edges with bobby pins. Then, she slipped into a T-shirt and faded blue chinos and added a woven belt and sneakers. The T had a silk screen of a cartoon pony on the front, and the words *I'm Just Horsing Around*. It was like one of Dad's dorky jokes, but Madison loved the purple color of the fabric, and the words were half faded and practically unreadable anyway, so she wore it.

Back in her room, in front of the gilt-edged mirror, Madison searched inside her jewelry box for the right pair of earrings to go with her outfit. She located a pair of dangly gold hoops and tried them on. But they were too long. Then she put on a pair of silver-studded flowers, but they pinched her ears. Finally, Madison settled on a simple pair of purple-beaded drop earrings to match her shirt. She posed in the mirror with the earrings, readjusting her bobby pins.

Higher up on the mirror were some odds and ends that had been taped there hastily over the past weeks and months: a postcard from Dad's and Stephanie's honeymoon, Mom's photo from the newspaper, a dried flower from Dad, a picture of

Phin, and a photo strip of Madison and Hart that they'd taken at the Far Hills Shoppes in one of those photo booths. Madison and Hart made different funny faces in each picture: pucker-ups, frowns, grins, and toothy smiles. In one of the pictures (Madison's personal favorite), Hart had his head turned to the side so it almost looked as if he were about to kiss her on the cheek.

Madison sprayed on some Flora, a fragrant floral body spray given to her by her stepmother. Stephanie was always indulging Madison with body creams, sprays, shampoos, candles, and things she said would help Madison to feel pretty and girlie. Mom didn't mind, as long as Madison didn't wear makeup or anything too sophisticated.

"For goodness' sakes, Maddie, you're only twelve!" was Mom's constant refrain. Madison wondered what would happen now that seventh grade was ending and thirteen was just around the corner. Would Mom's rules change just like everything else was changing?

Fully dressed, the rest of the house still asleep, Madison crept down to the kitchen with her laptop. She could make a bowl of cereal and check e-mail at the same time.

With her bowl of Corn Chex and berries, Madison sat at the table and powered up the computer. She was glad to have a wireless router. Her e-mailbox instantly came into view.

FROM	SUBJECT
⊠ BoopDeeDoop	Prom-O-Rama Sale
⊠ JeffFinn	Dinner!
⊠ First$$Mutual	Get Life Insurance NOW
⊠ AmericanDEX	Free Trial Offer
⊠ Dantheman	clinic SOS
⊠ Bigwheels	BTW
⊠ 889MovieLynx	screeningtimes
⊠ WillPOWR	Remember me?

Madison couldn't believe how jammed the mailbox had gotten since only the day before. She scanned for familiar names first. Dad had sent an e-mail confirming dinner with Stephanie for that Wednesday. Dan had sent more news about the changes at the Far Hills clinic. Even Bigwheels had dropped her a short note.

From: Bigwheels
To: MadFinn
Subject: BTW
Date: Mon 12 Jun 11:19 PM
Ok so I know HOW late it is and my
parents would bean me if they knew
I was up typing (WEIN?) But I
wanted to write and check in again
about that whole Ivy enemy fight ur
having. I thought of something else
u could do. U should send her an
anonymous note or something that
says u know she's cheating. That

way she'll get really paranoid. Is
that 2 much like something she'd
do? LMKWYT.

Yours till the family feuds (or
friend feuds, I guess),

Vicki aka Bigwheels

p.s.: Almost 4got: we're getting a
PONY!!! My dad and mom decided it
would be good therapy for all of us
to ride on the wkends. I'll tell u
more 18r. I have 2 think of a good
name for her--b/c it's a girl pony.
I know ur probably thinking we
already have 2 many pets but who
cares? LOL

Bye!

Madison chuckled. Bigwheels was getting another
pet? That was really no big surprise. She could practically start her own animal clinic somewhere in
Washington State.

After reading the familiar names, Madison
moved through the remainder of the e-mails, hitting
DELETE after each spam. She didn't recognize any
of these Web addresses, like First$$Mutual or
AmericanDEX. As for the ad from her favorite store,

Boop Dee Doop, Madison didn't feel like shopping just then. Before she could delete the last e-mail of the bunch, something made Madison stop. The e-mail had been written the night before, after midnight. Madison didn't know the screen name, WillPOWR, but for some reason, she thought it might be from a real person, not a spammer.

She was right.

Madison scanned the e-mail for viruses. When the message was cleared, she clicked on the text.

From: WillPOWR
To: MadFinn
Subject: Remember me?
Date: Tues 13 Jun 12:32 AM

Hey how r u? Do u even remember me?
I hope so. I met u @ Camp Sunshine
we were on the Egrets 2gether. I
live in NYC and said maybe we could
stay in touch but then I 4got to
write and I found this paper list
w/yr name on it so I thought I
would finally write & say hi. BTW I
have this great pic that someone
took of us and I have kept it all
this time. Actually, it's a picture
w/u, me, & that girl Ann. Remember
her? Did u keep in touch w/her? She
& I kept in touch a little bit but
I dunno. So if u get this and want

2 write back that would be kool. Do
u ever go into NYC? Where do u live
again? OK I better go, it's late.
Write back if you want.

Or not.

Will.

Madison felt her chest clench. Was this some kind
of joke?
Will? From camp? From Florida?
The e-mail gave new meaning to the word "flab-
bergasted." She reread it again and pictured Will's
shaggy blond hair. Cute. Right now he was an eighth
grader preparing for his own MUD; and next year he
would be a freshman, a ninth grader—one of the
"big" kids. And he wanted to get back in touch?
How could this not be a big, major, huge deal?
Madison hit REPLY right away. She started to type.

From: MadFinn
To: WillPOWR
Subject: Re: Remember me?
Date: Tues 13 Jun 7:19 AM
Thanks for writing. Wow, I was
surprised. I didn't think u would
remember me, but then you wrote and
I just felt so happy inside when I
was reading yr

"Ack! That's *terrible*," Madison groaned to herself as she quickly punched DELETE, DELETE, DELETE. She had to make absolutely sure those words didn't get sent to Will.

With another keystroke, Madison saved her reply to her "Drafts" folder. This was going to take some time. Madison would have to think extra-hard about how to respond without sounding like a dweeb.

The floor upstairs squeaked. Mom was up.

"Maddie?" Mom called out. "Are you awake?"

"Down here," Madison replied from the kitchen.

Yawning, Mom came down the stairs and shuffled into the kitchen wearing her slippers and a terry-cloth robe. Her hair was curly and damp; she had just towel-dried it.

"You're up so early today. And dressed! Trouble sleeping again, honey bear?" Mom said, yawning again.

Madison nodded and tried not to yawn herself. She pointed to Mom's head. "I didn't hear you take a shower," Madison said.

"That's because you're too focused on that laptop," Mom said with a sleepy wink. She walked over to the coffeemaker and started scooping some hazelnut roast into the gold filter.

"I got an e-mail," Madison blurted out.

Mom chuckled. "Just one? That is news. . . ."

"No," Madison said. "I got one e-mail that was different."

Mom got a worried look on her face. "*Bad* different?" she asked, moving toward Madison and the laptop. "Let me see."

"No, no," Madison said reassuringly. "Not bad. Not spam. Not dangerous."

"Oh," Mom said, taking a step back. "Then, how was it different?"

"It was from someone I haven't seen in a while," Madison said.

"Hmmm," Mom was thinking hard now. "Was it Stephanie's nephew in Texas? You said he was cute. Or maybe that boy from Chicago . . . You remember him, don't you?"

"Mo-o-o-o-om," Madison said, feeling her cheeks turn pink. Of course she remembered the boy from Chicago. Mark had given her her first kiss, on the Fourth of July at Gramma's lake house. Thoughts of him and fireworks still made Madison grin.

"Who wrote the e-mail?" Mom asked finally. She wasn't in the mood to guess anymore.

"Remember that guy Will I met at Camp Sunshine in Florida, when I was down there with Dad and Stephanie?"

"Will? Yes, I do remember. You e-mailed me about him. What did he say?"

"Hello. Good-bye. You know. He lives in Manhattan and wants to see me, or at least that's what he said," Madison replied.

"See you? My goodness!" Mom cried. "We'll

81

have to see about that, young lady. Maybe I can come along as chaperone. . . ."

Drrrinnngg!

Madison and Mom looked toward the doorway at the same moment. From somewhere in the house, Phinnie started to bark. He'd heard the doorbell, too.

"I wonder which one of your many admirers has come to see you this early?" Mom asked.

"Mom, quit teasing me!" Madison said. "I nearly forgot. It's Aimee. It's time for school."

Madison scrambled to toss her laptop, notebook, and the other things she needed for school into her orange bag. Then she slung the bag over her shoulder and headed for the kitchen door.

"One second. About that Will boy . . ." Mom said. "Did you answer his e-mail yet?"

Madison shook her head. "Not yet. But I want to."

"Before you do . . . let's discuss it . . . *seriously*," Mom said. "You know how I feel about online safety. And *boy* safety . . ."

"Okay, I know," Madison said as she kissed Mom on the cheek.

Madison turned and raced to the front door. Phin raced, too, panting as he went.

When she opened the door, Aimee and Fiona were standing on the porch.

"Good morning!" Aimee chirped. She sounded way more cheery than she usually did. Madison guessed that she'd had one of Mrs. Gillespie's veggie-protein shakes for breakfast.

"Hey, Aim, hey, Fiona," Madison said. She motioned them both to come inside for a moment while she kissed the dog good-bye. Then she yelled to her mom again.

"See you later, Mom!" Madison cried.

"Later!" Mom called.

The girls had taken only a few steps outside when Madison found herself unable to hold in her big, big news any longer.

"I have a secret!" Madison gushed.

"I already told Fiona about the Japan trip," Aimee said.

"You did?" Madison said, a little disappointed.

"I am wicked jealous. A trip to Asia sounds excellent," Fiona said. "Now you'll be a globe-trekker, just like Lindsay and Madhur."

"Can you believe it?" Madison cried. "But *that's* not the biggest secret."

"It's not?" Aimee asked.

Madison paused dramatically. "I got a mysterious e-mail from a boy," she admitted.

"What boy?" Fiona asked.

"It's not Hart?" Aimee asked.

Madison shook her head. "Nope."

"Is it from that guy you met out at your grandmother's house?" Fiona asked.

"No way! You haven't talked about him in

forever. What was his name again?" Aimee asked.

Madison could hardly get a word in edgewise. "No, it wasn't Mark. It was another boy I met, at Camp Sunshine in Florida."

"Turtle boy!" Aimee teased.

"His name was Will, right?" Fiona asked.

"Hold on. Didn't you fix him up with another girl when you were at camp?" Aimee said.

"Yeah! And didn't they hit it off?" Fiona added.

"I thought they liked each other," Madison said, "but now . . ."

"He likes *you*?" Fiona said. "Whoa. Complications!"

"He doesn't like you . . . he lo-o-o-o-oves you!" Aimee teased, gently slapping Madison on the back. The three friends tripped down the sidewalk laughing.

"So where does this leave Hart?" Fiona asked.

"What do you mean?" Madison asked in turn.

"Well, do you like Hart or this other guy Will more?" Fiona asked. "You have to decide."

"I like Hart. Totally," Madison said. "Duh, you know the answer to that."

"Of course that's what you'd say to us," Aimee quipped, "but you like this other guy, too, don't you? I can tell. Even if it is just a little. Your cheeks got all pink when you said his name."

"My cheeks are not pink! And I do not like Will more," Madison said.

"Maddie, it's nice that some guy likes you," Aimee said. "But . . ."

"But you can't ditch Hart for some turtle camp dude!" Fiona declared.

"You can't ditch the one guy who was so cool to you all throughout seventh grade. . . ." Aimee added.

"Ditch Hart?" Madison cried. "You guys are kidding, right? I'm not ditching anyone, especially not him. . . ."

"I think Hart is the nicest boy in our class," Fiona raved. "He'd be crushed if you blew him off. . . ."

"Fiona, stop saying that stuff!" Madison wailed. "I am not blowing him off."

Aimee rolled her eyes. *"Yet,"* she said bluntly. "You're not blowing him off *yet*."

There was silence on the sidewalk. Madison didn't know what to make of her friends' comments. Did they really think Madison was going to break up with Hart and ruin their perfect little group of pals?

Aimee pinched Madison on the shoulder. "Maddie, don't look so serious. We're just kidding," she said.

"Yeah, Maddie, don't worry. We know your true-blue feelings."

Madison laughed along with them, even though she didn't find any of their jokes very funny. How ridiculous of them to think that she'd throw Hart

Jones over! Even if they were kidding. It had taken Madison an entire seventh-grade year to gain Hart's affections, and she wasn't about to jeopardize that for some random kid from Camp Sunshine.

Was she?

Chapter 8

As Madison, Aimee, and Fiona approached the last block before school, talk of boys ceased, and talk of science and English homework commenced.

But Madison was still thinking about Will.

She would never admit it to her BFFs, but Madison *had* had a bit of a crush on Will at camp—and she knew that feelings like that didn't evaporate, no matter who was involved. Maybe there still was something between her and him. . . .

Guilt, guilt. Twinge, twinge.

It was hard not to wonder about the possibility. . . .

After getting her books out of her locker, Madison headed off to Mr. Danehy's room. Almost immediately, she ran into Hart.

Guilt, guilt. Twinge, twinge.

"I saw you walking," Hart said.

"What's up?" Madison asked, biting her lip.

Hart gave her a funny look. "Nothing much."

Madison bit her lip again. One of her occasional weaknesses was that of showing utterly transparent facial expressions. What if Hart saw right through the forced smile, all the way to the guilty twinge that lurked beneath?

"I'm so-o-o-o great," Madison said. "Really."

I am such a bad liar, she thought.

Hart shifted uncomfortably from one foot to the other, hands in pockets, backpack on his shoulder. Why was *he* acting so strange?

Madison was about to say something positive and upbeat about Hart's T-shirt when she was bumped from behind.

"Excuse *me*," Poison Ivy Daly huffed, pushing past them.

"Now *that* was uncool," Hart said disdainfully.

"We'd better get seated or Mr. Danehy will freak," Madison said, nudging Hart with her elbow.

Hart took his seat over by Chet, who was scribbling something into his notebook. Madison veered toward the stool next to Poison Ivy.

"So, Mr. Danehy knows how you've been acting toward me," Ivy growled.

Madison wanted to jump up on the lab counter and scream, "Oh, yeah? Well what would that be, Miss Stinky-pants Traitor-girl?"

But she said nothing.

"Did you hear me?" Ivy growled again. "I said that I—"

"Yes, I heard you," Madison said softly. "The whole planet can hear when you talk. You don't have to bark."

Madison sat back, satisfied with her retort. Lately, she'd been rich in sassy comebacks. She felt pleased knowing that Ivy's feathers would be permanently ruffled for the entire length of the class.

As if on cue, Ivy leaned back, away from Madison's stool, and let out an enormous squawk. Everyone heard it, including the teacher.

"Is there a problem, Ms. Daly?" Mr. Danehy asked from the front of the room. It was his usual question.

"No," Ivy said, glaring right at Madison.

"Oh, yeah, everything's just hunky-dory-doo," Madison quipped under her breath.

"Excuse me?" Ivy asked.

Madison looked Ivy straight in the eye. "Would you just chill out?" she said. "We have to get this project done somehow. There's no escape, and you're not helping."

For some reason, Ivy didn't have a comeback this time. She just stared at Madison.

Madison took advantage of the silence. "Just take a look at the notes, will you?" she asked, shoving her notebook back at Ivy. "According to you, this notebook is part yours, anyhow, right?"

Ivy nodded. "Fine."

Madison flipped through the pages where she'd drawn diagrams and scribbled ideas. Although she expected continued enemy resistance, Ivy seemed okay with the "Why Is the Sky Blue?" topic. She looked and listened and . . . who says miracles can't happen in science classrooms? She started acting like a partner.

Shocking.

Actually, the pair didn't have much of a choice as to whether or not to agree. Mr. Danehy made their minds up for them. He roamed the classroom like a lion on the prowl, asking for topics *or* offering ultimatums. If the students didn't choose a subject on their own, he chose one for them with a loud, king-of-the-jungle roar, naturally. Madison knew there was no fate worse than letting a teacher pick your project topic. If it were up to Mr. Danehy, Madison figured that she and Ivy would end up doing some complex physics equation that was impossible to decipher. They'd both be sunk.

Of course, agreeing on the topic as partners didn't keep Ivy from making dumb, obnoxious comments throughout the class.

"This is the stupidest plan I've ever planned."

"Is the sky the only thing that's considered sky blue?"

"Come on! I can see gamma rays. Can't you?"

Madison tried to ignore most of Ivy's lame

remarks. She huddled close to the enemy, sketching the electromagnetic spectrum and angles of refracted light—all things that helped to explain the question at hand.

"According to Mr. Danehy's directions, we need to use the scientific method to answer our question," Madison explained.

"What's the scientific method? Wait a minute, we totally did *not* cover this in class," Ivy groaned.

"Chapter twelve," Madison insisted. "We just talked about it last week."

"Well, I must have been absent," Ivy said, making one of her typical excuses. "I would have remembered this."

Yeah, right.

"How are we doing over here?" Mr. Danehy asked, coming up behind Madison and Ivy.

"Greater than great," Madison said with a sigh. "We're working together in perfect harmony."

"Harmony, huh?" Mr. Danehy repeated. He didn't look convinced, so Madison added, "We were just covering some hot topics."

"Yes, I was just telling Madison about the electromagnetic spectrum and visible light," Ivy said.

Madison's jaw dropped. She wanted to kick Ivy.

"Visible light? That sounds quite good," Mr. Danehy said, sounding semi-impressed by Ivy's comments.

"And that's not all. We have this major experiment planned to prove how the color blue appears and how light is refracted."

Madison felt the tips of her ears turn scarlet with anger. What a sucker punch. Ivy had totally read her notes and then recited them like they were her own. The nerve!

For the remainder of class, Ivy and Madison "shared" more ideas and notes. Ivy, of course, continued to gloat. At one point, she even passed a note over to her drones. Madison guessed that it said something unkind about Madison.

When the end-of-class bell rang, Hart ambled over. Ivy spoke to him as she got up from her stool. "Hello, Hart," she said.

"Hello," Hart replied, trying to move out of her path.

"Did you get my invitation?" Ivy asked.

Hart shrugged. "No. What invitation?"

Ivy rolled her eyes and leaned toward him. "My mother is throwing this mega event at the end of school. Everyone will be there."

She shot a look at Madison.

"Well," Ivy said softly, "almost everyone."

"I have plans," Hart said without missing a beat.

"But . . . you don't even know the time or place. Look, just read my invitation and let me know," Ivy said, as if she hadn't even heard him say no.

As soon as Ivy had strutted out of the room,

Madison mimed throwing up.

"She makes me so, *so* sick," Madison said, rubbing her tummy.

"Me, too," Hart said.

"Are you going to the soccer game today?" Madison asked.

Hart shook his head. "No can do. I have to meet my dad after school. Wish Fiona luck for me, okay? And E me or IM me later."

"Okay," Madison said, watching him disappear into the throng of kids flooding the hall between classes.

The soccer match was set to begin right after the final school bell. Madison knew she wanted to get to the field quickly, not only because of the large crowd, but also because Far Hills was playing against its bitter rival, Dunn Manor. Madison was in the mood for rivalry. After all, she'd been living it throughout her classes all day long. Why should after-school events be any different?

After dumping a few books back in her locker, Madison searched the hallway for someone with whom to walk over to the soccer field. Madhur and Aimee were talking near the girls' bathroom.

The three of them headed over together.

"Give me an M-A-L-L-A-R-D!" cried the opposing team's cheering section.

Madison and her friends clapped loudly to drown

out the cheer, and clapped even more loudly when Fiona and her teammates took to the field.

Normally, a soccer game would not have been so well attended. But the scores had been close all year long. These last games of the season were the deciding ones: who would walk away as the soccer champs? Everyone at Far Hills wanted to be a part of the girls'-soccer-team triumph.

Madison scanned the bleachers for a sign of Hart. Although he had said he wouldn't be at the game, there was always the off chance he'd changed his mind. But he wasn't out there. She did see Dan, however; he came right over to where she and the other girls sat.

"Hey!" Dan said. "I e-mailed you, like, ten times this week, Maddie."

"No," Madison said. "It was once or twice, and I e-mailed you back."

"You did not," Dan said. "I didn't get it."

"Since when do you get anything—except the extra slice of pizza?" Aimee teased. Dan's nickname back in elementary school had been Pork-O, because he'd had a reputation for eating everyone's snacks and leftovers. Here it was the end of seventh grade, and he still couldn't live it down.

"Go, Rangers!" kids in the stands shouted as a whistle blew.

The game was starting.

Madison waved to Fiona as she stepped on the

field in her blue-and-white uniform. Shin guards poked up through the tops of her socks, and her cleats looked new, even from a distance. She looked a little like her idol, Mia Hamm, with her ponytail. Madison had learned a lot about women's soccer just from the posters that lined Fiona's bedroom wall. And from games like this.

"*Go, Fiona!*" Madison squealed, although she was pretty sure Fiona wouldn't hear with all the noise. Still, it was luckier than lucky to cheer right out loud for a friend.

"This is my favorite thing at school," Madhur gushed, clapping wildly.

"Soccer?" Madison asked.

"No," Madhur said. "Being a part of something so much bigger than me. That's how I feel about most things. You don't get it at school when you're taking some English test. But you do get it here, in the middle of everything."

Madison had to nod, since she liked being in the middle of everything, too.

At the end of the row where the girls and Dan sat, Madison saw some guys approaching. Hart was not among them, but Drew, Egg, and Chet were.

As soon as Chet saw Madhur, he came closer and took a seat in the row directly ahead of her. Madison saw them flirt. She knew the signs only too well from observing Ivy's moves and knowing how she herself acted in similar situations.

Back out on the field, the game wasn't producing any goals—yet.

But all that was about to change.

Fiona and her teammate Daisy Espinoza set themselves up at midfield for a pass. Fiona had to kick the ball upfield to beat a defender, but when she got it back again, she was able to launch it with a high kick. It traveled all the way downfield toward the Mallard goalie. Everyone raced to beat it. The crowd went wild.

"I can't believe what a good game this is," Egg said.

"For girls' soccer, you mean?" Dan said.

"Hey!" Madison elbowed Dan in the side. "Watch it. Why wouldn't girls' soccer be good?"

"I was being a doof," Dan admitted, elbowing Madison right back. "But Egg is the one who always rags on Fiona and her teammates. Not me."

"Sorry," Madison said. She had taken her girl power a little too far.

Back on the turf, the opposing team's goalie picked up the ball and threw it off to the side to a teammate. But as luck would have it, Super-Fiona was right there, her feet moving as fast as could be. She intercepted the ball and dribbled it quickly downfield.

Then something crazy happened: Fiona tripped.

Or, as Egg would later complain, "She was gypped! She was tripped!"

Everyone watched as Fiona fell to the ground and then got back up again, limping. Luckily, her ankle did not appear to be sprained; it was just that she had been momentarily stunned. Even better, the Mallards weren't able to regain possession of the ball. Fiona soon had the ball again and this time dribbled it off to Daisy, who booted it right into the net. As the ball sailed high over the opposing goalie's head, everyone rooting for the Far Hills Rangers let out a roar.

"That makes ten goals this season for Daisy," Aimee said. She knew all the stats. Fiona had been explaining the facts and figures to her online just the other day.

"And eight assists this year for Fiona, too, right?" Madison added.

Aimee and Madison gave each other a high five. BFFs always knew the important details.

In the final minutes of the game, the Dunn Manor Mallards came back with an amazing goal, but it was too late to do any serious damage. Far Hills was already ahead by four goals at that point. The final score: 4–1, Far Hills Rangers.

"I'm so glad you didn't get hurt," Madison told Fiona when they all met up on a grassy mound near the main school building after the game. As usual, Fiona brushed off everyone's concerns. She always did that when it came to injuries or anything that got in the way of her and soccer. Nothing could ever keep her from the game she loved so much.

Everyone threw their bags down on the grass and lay back, gazing up at the blue sky. Madison smiled to herself. At that moment, she felt much closer to knowing—*really knowing*—why that sky overhead was the color it was. And it didn't have to do just with the spectrum and science projects. It had to do with the friends sitting nearby.

"You're all going on the field trip, right?" Aimee asked aloud.

"No doubt," Madison said.

"Ooops!" Fiona cried. "I forgot to get my permission slip signed. I think Chet forgot, too."

"You still have a day," Aimee said.

"Good," Fiona said. "I think it'll be a fun afternoon."

"I heard they're planning rowboat races this year," Aimee said.

"Really?" Madison cried. She had a picture in her mind: her and Hart seated in the center of a red rowboat, Hart rowing, and Madison sunning herself. It was perfection, like something in a movie.

After a while everyone stood up and said their good-byes for the afternoon. As they walked off, Madison noticed how Chet and Madhur strolled side by side. They seemed to be spending more and more time together these days. Of course, Fiona and Egg walked side by side, too, as usual. All Madison could think about was Hart and how much she would have liked to be by his side.

Aimee must have sensed that Madison was getting a little melancholy, because she linked arms with her BFF and leaned close.

"I hope Fiona doesn't move back to California," Aimee said. "This year with the three of us has been the best."

Madison looked over at her friend and sighed. Aimee was so right.

She felt a pang inside, knowing somehow that when things seemed very good . . . like right now . . . *that* was when everything began to shift. It was some kind of unwritten law of life.

"I hope she doesn't move, either," Madison said back to Aimee. "I don't want things to change—not ever."

And then Aimee and Madison hugged, right there in the middle of the sidewalk, right there in front of everyone.

Because that's what best friends forever are supposed to do.

Chapter 9

On Tuesday evening, Madison lay stretched across her bed with her feet dangling off the edge. She rolled over and raised her legs straight up in the air. Mosquito bites lined her shins, and it wasn't even really summer yet.

Plus, Madison really needed a pedicure. The carnation pink–colored polish from her previous one was wearing off. Maybe she and Aimee could paint each other's toenails this week. They did that sometimes up in Aimee's bedroom, or outside, in Aimee's little rooftop hideaway. It was one of their favorite girl things to do. In addition to being the world's best hair-braider, Aimee was a brilliant nail-polisher.

Phin sprawled nearby, little paws in the air, snoring (and drooling) on a pillow.

After a long day of classes, the Rangers-Mallards soccer game, and a Thai food takeout night with Mom, Madison wasn't in the mood to do anything, especially anything that had to do with school. So she fluctuated between homework and no work. Instead of science chapters, Madison dived in to some back issues of *Star Beat* magazine. The purple science notebook that Ivy had claimed as her own lay open in front of Madison, its pages filled with notes from class and Internet research on the project.

But appearances were deceiving.

Many of the margins were crammed with non-science doodles.

Boy doodles.

In lieu of writing science formulas, Madison was making up boy-girl formulas. It was like being matchmaker and matched all in one.

She scribbled down her own name and the names of boys she knew: boys like Hart (of course); Egg (just because he'd been around forever); Dan (because they had so much in common); and yes, even Will (now back on the scene). Then she counted the number of *A*'s, *E*'s, *I*'s, *O*'s, and *U*'s in each person's name. Finally, she counted the vowels in her own name. If the totals for both names matched, she decided, she was a good match for that person.

HART & MADISON = One match . . .
WALTER & MADISON = One match . . .
DAN & MADISON = One match . . .
WILLIAM & MADISON = Two matches?

Madison glanced around the room upon her discovery of the fact that Will was the best match, at least in this version of matchmaking; it was as if someone were there, spying, peering over her shoulder. . . .

That twinge in her stomach was back again.

She instantly thought of Will's screen name. WillPOWR.

Boy, did she need some of that right now.

Willpower.

Madison didn't need to like anyone else. She had all the "like" she needed with Hart. Right? Madison clicked her e-mailbox. It was time to reread Will's e-mail and finally respond. Although it had been a whole day, Madison still didn't know what to write. Or at least she didn't know what to write that didn't sound stupid, with a capital *S*.

Cluck, cluck, cluck.

She started making funny noises. She felt like such a chicken: afraid to write one e-mail; afraid that Hart might find out that Madison "sort of" liked someone else; and afraid that the end of seventh grade was turning into some kind of mini-melodrama.

"Maddie?"

Mom knocked and walked right in, as usual. No surprises there. Privacy was an unknown concept in that house, especially lately. Ever since Madison had started liking and seeing a boy, Mom had become exponentially nosier.

"You busy?" Mom asked.

Phin woke up with a start. He jumped off the bed and raced over toward Mom's ankles, his tongue flapping.

"Hello, Phinnie," Mom said, scooping up the pug.

"I'm trying to do homework," Madison said tersely. "That's why my door was shut."

"I'm sure you were," Mom said. "I just wanted to tell you that I spoke to my boss at Budge today."

Madison perked up. "You did? What did he say?"

Mom came over with Phin and sat on the edge of the bed.

"He said I should book my tickets to Kyushu," Mom said.

"Where's that? I thought you were going to Japan," Madison said.

"Honey bear, Kyushu is an island in southern Japan. The world's largest double volcano is there."

"Wow," Madison said. "*Double* volcano? And I can really come with you to see it?"

"Yes," Mom nodded, "either to Kyushu or maybe to Geibikei Gorge, in northern Japan. We'll see. I have a lot of organizing and planning to do in a very short time."

"Wow," Madison said again. "Japan! Somebody, pinch me!"

Mom leaned over and pinched Madison ever so gently on the forearm. Then she kissed Madison's forehead.

Before either one could push the dog back, Phin jumped between the two, drooling. Madison's purple notebook and everything else on Madison's bed flew onto the carpet.

It was a big mess, but Madison couldn't help but giggle at the pile. Phin had tumbled right off the bed, too, landing right on top of everything else.

"Rowowooorroooo!"

"I like knowing we'll have some quality time together this summer," Mom said to Madison.

"Me, too," Madison said. She glanced down at Phinnie, and he stared right back into her eyes.

"Don't look at me like that," Madison said to her doggy. Then she looked at Mom. "Look at Phin's eyes, Mom," she said. "He knows we're planning something and that he can't come."

"Rowowooorroooo!"

Phin scratched at the carpet and made a 360-degree turn, as if he were chasing his little pug tail. Mom and Madison both laughed.

It really did seem as though Phinnie understood every single word they said.

"Good morning, students!" boomed Assistant Principal Goode's voice.

Kids covered their ears as microphone static sizzled over the public-address system. "We have a few special announcements for today, Wednesday, June fourteenth," Mrs. Goode continued. "As you know, school is winding down, but our school calendar is as jam-packed as ever. I hope everyone brought home all the flyers we distributed with information and dates for field trips, graduation, and—don't forget—special performances. . . ."

Madison glanced across the room at Hart. She was thinking again about how cool he'd been to give up performing in the musical revue just so he could join Madison backstage.

So-o-o-o-o cool.

Hart stared back. It looked as though he might have even winked, but Madison knew that that was just sunlight in his eyes. Still, he looked as cute as ever.

And he was cuter, way *cuter than Will*, she kept telling herself.

Madison turned her head and gazed out of the windows along the side of the room. The afternoon sun made the whole sky look white. For a moment, Madison felt her eyes close as though she were being swallowed up by all the light.

It was warmer than warm in there.

Kids whispered as Mrs. Goode droned on and on, her voice loud and insistent. For some reason, none of the words seemed to make any sense to Madison.

The conversation was unintelligible, like white noise. Madison felt as if she were sinking into quicksand. She wasn't in the classroom anymore; she was somewhere outside that scene, somewhere familiar, but somewhere *else*.

She was dreaming.

Madison saw herself dressed up in a short skirt (she'd never had one), tank top (she'd never worn one), and lace-up sandals (surprisingly like the ones Poison Ivy wore). But despite the strangeness of the image, Madison didn't question the outfit or the thoughts. She just walked down the hall at school, and everyone—*everyone*—stopped to talk or wave or just stare. It was as if Madison had been wearing a neon sign that read, MOST POPULAR. Her hair was pulled back in a braided bun, secured with a rhinestone hair clip and barrettes. She wore a long beaded necklace and carried a bohemian bag made from vintage fabric. When other students stopped to greet her, they complimented her on her bag or her shoes or some other aspect of her outfit.

While walking down the hall, Madison saw herself approach Dan Ginsburg, who stood at his locker. But in this daydream, Dan was skinnier and taller. He wasn't Pork-O at all.

Wow.

"Hey, Maddie," Dan said in a smoother than smooth voice.

"Hey," Madison replied, tossing her hair.

"Are you coming to the clinic this week?" Dan asked.

"You bet," Madison said.

"You sure you won't go to the movies with me this Saturday?" Dan asked hopefully.

Madison grinned. "I'm sure." Then she continued her walk down the hall. She turned a corner. There, she nearly collided with Chet Waters.

"Hey, Maddie," Chet said, speaking with the same smooth tones that Dan had used.

"Hey," Madison said, cocking her hip to one side and slinging her trendy bag over the opposite shoulder.

"Are you absolutely, positively sure you won't go to the mall with me this Saturday?" Chet asked. It was more like begging.

Madison shook her head. "Another time, Chetty."

Chetty?

What kind of a nickname was *that*?

Madison kept right on walking, straight down the hallway. Other kids stopped and stared. What was everyone looking at? They weren't looking at her, were they?

"Yo, Maddie!"

Madison stopped short in front of Egg. He blocked her path. For the first time in the daydream, here was something expected: Egg, getting in the way. But he was taller than usual. And nicer. And cuter, too. Strangely, Fiona was nowhere to be seen.

"What's up with the plan to hang out on Saturday and play computer games?" Egg asked.

Madison bowed her head coyly and looked in the opposite direction. "No plan, man," Madison replied, making a ridiculous rhyme that somehow sounded flirtatious.

Flirting with Egg? This really was unreal.

After Egg stepped aside, Madison walked on. A few yards farther down the hall, she saw Drew, and then Hart, both standing close by their lockers.

Drew waved but didn't say anything. Instead, he handed Madison a note on purple paper. A note! Madison opened it.

Want to come over Saturday for a pool party? You can be my extraspecial guest. We can do karaoke.

Madison crumpled up the note and tossed it at his feet, shaking her head.

"May-beee," she said in a teasing voice. It didn't sound like her actual voice, either. It was more as though she were talking through her nose, not her mouth. Or singing.

Wait a minute. Madison couldn't sing.

Hart stepped up to Madison and took her by the elbow.

"I know we've got plans tonight, right?" Hart asked, cocking his head. "Everyone's going to the movies, and so are we."

"We are?" Madison laughed.

Hart looked surprised at her response. Madison had never seen him look that way before.

Then, she realized that she wasn't standing there alone with Hart. Everyone in school was right there, right behind her, following close, close on her heels. There were Ivy, Rose, Joanie, Dan, Drew, Chet . . . *everyone* . . . except Aimee or Fiona or Lindsay or Madhur . . .

"Is there a problem?" Madison said as she turned to face the crowd.

Everyone rushed toward Madison. It was a whoosh of noise and faces and smiles and frowns and, oh, my goodness, how woozy she felt as the crowd pushed closer.

Then, as if by magic, everyone froze.

An unfamiliar voice called out from behind one of the classroom doors.

"Over here, Maddie!" the voice cried.

Who was there?

When she glanced over in the direction of the voice, Madison saw a stranger. It was Will.

What was Will doing at Far Hills Junior High?

"Maddie!"

What was she supposed to say to him? And why was he yelling?

"Will you snap out of it?"

Madison blinked hard a few times. She shook her head. She was no longer inside the daydream. She was back in homeroom. And Egg—not Will—was the one yelling.

"Quit spacing out, Maddie," Egg barked. He poked her in the arm for the umpteenth time.

"What's going on?" Madison asked, rubbing her arm and checking it for bruises.

Egg looked concerned. He lowered his voice. "Are you okay, Maddie?"

"I think so," Madison said. She looked down to see what she was actually wearing. *Whew.* No short skirt. No tank. No sandals. She had on faded jeans, a cotton shirt, and sneaker-mules, just as always.

"Whoa," Madison said, squinting at Egg. "Now that was truly weird."

"Yeah, I guess so. You never zoned out like that before," Egg said. "The announcements are over. First period is about to start."

"Oh," Madison said, still feeling the ripples of her daydream. "I guess I was just thinking about stuff."

"What was so funny?" Egg asked.

"Funny?"

"You were smiling," Egg said. "Wacko."

"Don't call me names," Madison said.

"I always call you names. It's what I do."

Madison rolled her eyes and scanned the room. Egg had witnessed her entire daydream episode. Had anyone else in class seen her space out as though she'd traveled all the way to Venus and back?

She clutched her chest, taking shallow little breaths. Never had such a vivid daydream or night dream happened in Madison's life. It was like watching a crazy movie.

Brrrinnnggg!

The bell for first class rang out, and Madison jumped, startled.

Egg jumped, too.

"Why did you jump like that?" Egg cried. "Stop it! You're freaking me out today, Maddie!"

"I guess that's just what I do," Madison said.

Egg groaned. "Hardy-har-*har*. You're a real laugh riot."

"Aw, just leave me alone," Madison grumbled.

She stood up with her orange bag, checking to make sure that she had all the right books for the morning classes. Science was first, and her purple science notebook was right there. Madison had been sure to rip out the doodle pages and to scratch out any incriminating names or games, but she quickly double-checked, just to make sure. She couldn't risk Ivy's spotting the words "Madison Jones" or "Madison + Will?" in the margin, now, could she?

Between the doodles and the crazy daydream, Madison was beginning to feel that her secret thoughts were getting the better of her.

At the same time, she just didn't know how to turn them off.

Chapter 10

By the end of the day on Wednesday, Madison was still preoccupied with boy thoughts. And it didn't help that her last class was Mrs. Wing's computer lab. Half the boys from the wild daydream were in that classroom.

Madison attempted to keep a low profile. She sat behind one of the computer monitors with a tight-lipped, blank expression on her face, trying very hard not to encourage any random conversations, especially not with Egg. No matter what the day or situation, Egg would find some sneaky way to slip under Madison's skin and drive her crazy. Today, she wasn't in the mood.

Sometimes Egg could be as nasty as Poison Ivy,

like a bad rash that wouldn't go away, teasing Madison relentlessly. Of course, he usually apologized in the end, but that didn't make his annoying behavior any easier to take.

"Hey," Egg grunted. "Are you ignoring me or what?"

Madison bit her tongue. She was *not* going to answer.

"Hey," Egg said a little louder. "I know you can he-e-e-e-ear me."

Not only could Madison hear him, she could feel his spit as he hurled comments her way.

"Shhhh!" she finally said, holding a finger up to her lips for emphasis. "We're supposed to be doing site updates, not talking."

Before Egg had a chance to say anything else, Madison was rescued by Mrs. Wing and a blue folder.

"Maddie," Mrs. Wing said sweetly, handing the folder to Madison, "I have a few memory pages that I need inputted into the database. Would you be able to handle this before class gets out?"

"Of course," Madison replied. "I'll input them right now."

Mrs. Wing handed a folder to Egg, too. He turned back to his computer and began to type.

Madison's folder contained at least five new handwritten memory-page profiles from other students in the seventh grade. Much to her surprise, the first page inside the folder was from Joan Kenyon, super drone. Madison immediately read through the text to see just what this friend of the queen of mean had written. But nothing in the profile seemed funny or strange or even mean. In fact, Phony Joanie came across as the sweetest, most unphony person on the planet.

As if.

Madison briefly considered what would happen if she were to alter Joan's page while inputting it on the computer. What if she changed a few words here and there, just to make Joan sound more like the mean drone she really was?

Madison giggled. First there were boy-crazy daydreams. Now she was having fleeting fantasies about getting drone revenge. Of course, it was all just fantasy. Madison wouldn't change a word of the profile. Changing the text was something *Ivy* would have done, not Madison.

When the end-of-day bell rang, Madison avoided all the guys and hustled to gather her belongings. The rehearsal for backstage help was about to begin downstairs. Kids who helped with props had practice in one room, while kids who were performing songs and dances practiced in another.

Hart was right there in Madison's rehearsal room, waiting. She walked over to him. Something seemed wrong. He wasn't making eye contact.

"How are you?" Madison asked gently, slipping

into the seat next to him.

"Fine, I guess, considering . . ." he grumbled.

"Considering . . . *what*?" Madison asked.

"Aw, you know," Hart said. He still wouldn't look her in the eye.

I know? Madison thought.

Madison clenched her stomach muscles.

Um . . . no, I don't know.

What was he talking about? Could he read her thoughts? Had Fiona or Aimee spilled the beans? Did Hart know about Will's e-mail?

"You look a little weird today," Hart commented, unaware of Madison's internal freak-out.

"I do?"

"Okay, not really."

"Oh."

How awkward. What was going on?

"Yeah . . . well . . . um . . ." Hart couldn't seem to get any words out. "I thought I would like to help with props and backstage work, but the truth is . . . well . . . I wish I was singing or dancing instead."

"But you said you wanted to be with me. . . ."

"I know," Hart replied, "and I thought I meant it, but I was thinking about it all day and . . . I changed my mind. I'm really sorry. . . ."

"It's okay, I guess," Madison said, trying to sound agreeable, even though she felt a little put off by Hart's change of heart. Was something else going on—and getting between them?

No, no, stop overthinking, Madison told herself. *He's just telling you what he really feels, and you're blowing the whole thing right out of proportion. . . .*

Madison tried to calm herself down. Up on stage, Mr. Montefiore tapped his foot and worked with the team of janitors as they hung the highest of the track lights. Madison watched them. It was better than watching Hart. He was acting so distant. Was this karmic payback for the Will e-mail and for all of Madison's daydreams?

At the end of the revue meeting, Madison and Hart said their good-byes, and Madison headed back to her locker. Her brain was exhausted from all the overthinking. She needed a BFF or a keypal connection right now, something that would screw her head back on straight.

Kids mingled in the hallways cleaning out old textbooks, notebooks, and locker decorations. Principal Bernard had designated this Locker Cleanup Day, and Madison had a lot of cleaning left to do. It was a good thing, too, just the thing to get Madison's mind off Hart.

But when she opened her locker, the first thing she saw was a photo of herself with Aimee, Fiona, Chet, and—guess who?—pasted on the inside. Everyone in the photo was sticking out his or her tongue in a goofy pose. Hart had his eyes crossed, too. That had been a fun day.

Seventh grade had seemed so uncomplicated before the "boy" got added to "friend."

"Hey, Maddie," someone said, strolling up beside Madison. It was Madhur; arms filled with papers and books. "My locker is such a sty," she complained.

"Mine, too," Madison said. As she reached inside, a pile of things fell out.

"Didn't you have revue rehearsal today?" Madhur asked.

Madison nodded. "Yes. You did, too, right?"

"Down in the basement. And it was seriously lame. All the performers were right there, but no one sang or danced. The downstairs piano was out of tune. What a waste of time."

"If it makes you feel any better," Madison said, "ours was lame, too. I was thinking maybe I would drop out."

"Drop out?" Madhur said. She sounded genuinely shocked.

"I think maybe I'll quit. I don't see the point," Madison said. "I have so much else to do."

"Quit? No way!" Madhur said. "You are *not* dropping out of the revue. It's our last big show of the year."

"Well," Madison mused. "I don't feel like much of a show-*off*."

"You have to stay in the show," Madhur said. "I am your friend, and I say so."

Madison laughed. "Huh? What are you? The boss of me?"

Madhur nodded. "Absolutely. And those are the rules."

"The rules?" Madison said, still laughing.

Aimee came over, followed by Fiona.

"Locker cleanup stinks," Aimee declared, pinching her nose for effect.

"They should just let us toss everything in a pile and light it with a match," Fiona said.

"Can we put Ivy in the pile, too?" Aimee said.

Madhur laughed.

"You should have seen *her* at rehearsal today," Aimee said to Madison.

"What happened?" Madison asked.

"She stood onstage to dance for one of the group numbers. Midway through the song, she fell flat on her nose. I swear, I heard it crunch."

"No-o-o-o!" Fiona said.

Madhur laughed again. "The classic Poison Ivy moment," she quipped.

"Wish I'd been there," Madison said.

"One very weird thing happened, though," Aimee continued. "Hart came in to our rehearsal at the very end to talk to the teacher-adviser."

"So?" Madison asked.

"So, why was he coming into the performers' meeting? Isn't he in the backstage group?"

Madison looked down at the linoleum floor. "I don't know."

"Wait," Aimee said. "Hart specifically told me he

was doing props so he could hang with you more before the end of school. He hasn't switched groups, has he?"

"So what if he has?" Madison asked.

"That makes no sense," Aimee said.

Madison just shrugged again. "Does anything make sense these days?"

Madhur and Aimee shrugged back. Then each girl returned to her locker to finish with cleanup. Madison glanced around to see if Lindsay might walk by, but she didn't see her.

Someone else came up to her, though. It was Mariah, and her pink streaks were back again, although they were a little lighter this time.

"Nice hair," Madison said.

"I couldn't resist, even though the teachers will probably make me change it again," Mariah said. "But my hair looks so boring when it's the natural color."

"I wish I had the guts to change my hair color," Madison said.

"Why? You have gorgeous hair just like it is," Mariah said.

"Thanks."

"I can't believe you guys are going to be in eighth grade soon," Mariah said.

"I can't believe you're going to be in high school," Madison said. "Are you scared?"

Mariah quickly replied, "No way!" and burst into a laugh.

Madison gave her a quizzical look. "You're not?"

"Okay, maybe a little, just like any year in a new class or school. But I'm psyched to meet some new kids, too."

"I'm so scared about next year, and I don't know why," Madison admitted.

"What else is up?" Mariah asked, raising an eyebrow. "Boy trouble?"

"Boys?" Madison said. "Me? No way."

"You are *so* lying," Mariah said, nudging Madison. "Come on, you can tell me. I know how to keep a secret. I swear."

"Okay," Madison confided. "There is one boy. We've known each other since we were kids. . . ."

"Oh, yeah?" Mariah smiled. "So, what about him?"

Madison looked away. "It's been this crush forever and ever. And it's mutual . . . but then there's this *other* guy who just showed up."

"Another guy?" Mariah asked. "Hmmm."

"He lives in New York City. I met him at turtle camp."

"Turtle camp?" Mariah said, holding back her giggles.

"That's what I called it. It was actually Camp Sunshine. Anyway," Madison continued, "the point is: I'm stuck."

"Does Forever Guy know about Turtle Camp Guy?" Mariah asked, giggling again.

"Well, not exactly . . . not like *that* . . ."

"Forever Guy is cool," Mariah replied. "He'll always like you, no matter what. Trust me."

"How do you know that?" Madison asked.

"Because my brother is totally predictable," Mariah said.

"Your brother?" Madison pinched her lips together in a frown. "Egg?"

"Yeah, that's who you're talking about, right? I mean, Egg is Forever Guy."

"Egg?" Madison's eyes got very wide.

"You've known each other since you were born, right?"

"Yeah, but . . ." Madison let out a little gasp. "Um . . . I was actually talking about Hart Jones," she explained. "*He's* Forever Guy."

"Oh, really? He is?" Mariah said, cool as a cucumber. "Well, I'm an idiot, then. I just thought . . . Sorry."

"You don't really think Egg has a crush on *me*, do you?" Madison asked.

"Nah, nah, nah," Mariah said. "I was just thinking out loud. I mean, we both know how much he digs Fiona."

"Yeah," Madison said, feeling much better. "I know she likes him."

"Hey, Maddie!" Fiona came over to where Madison and Mariah stood and poked her head between them. "And what are you two blabbing about?" she asked.

Mariah, who was almost never at a loss for words, inhaled sharply, somehow rendered speechless by Fiona's sudden appearance. She started to mumble something, but then stopped, waved, and started to walk away.

"Mariah?" Madison called out, but she disappeared around a corner.

"What's the matter with *her*?" Fiona asked.

"Er . . . stomachache," Madison said, lying to cover up.

"Did Mariah say anything about the field trip tomorrow?" Fiona asked.

"No," Madison said. "She wasn't talking about school."

"What was she talking about?"

"You," Madison said with a nervous giggle.

"Me?" Fiona said, looking worried. "Why would she be talking about me?"

"I'm just kidding," Madison said. "She was talking about her stomachache, I swear."

"Okay, so why were you laughing? Stomachaches aren't that funny."

"No, but life is," Madison said. "And we were just saying . . . seventh grade has been pretty hysterical, don't you think? Like . . . did you think your brother Chet would *ever* admit to liking a girl? And what about your bee sting episode in the spring? And Ivy Daly as class president? Puh-leez . . ."

Madison went on and on, still trying to cover up

for the fact that she'd just been talking about Fiona. It seemed weird. Like she had been backstabbing her BFF.

"I guess maybe you're right. Seventh grade has been funny," Fiona said.

Madison pushed her lips out, making a goofy face. "Funny!" she cried.

Fiona let out a laugh.

Then she and Madison ambled down the hall together, arm in arm, heading for Aimee's locker.

Chapter 11

The pig alarm clock oinked, and Madison rubbed her eyes. She was awake almost immediately, keyed up about the field trip.

The field-trip *outfit*, however, left Madison a little less excited. The greenish brown, fatigue-style capris she'd selected the night before were a little snug around the hips. Plus, she wasn't sure they were "weather appropriate." The skies outside were more gray than blue, which meant there was a chance of showers, which also meant she should probably be dressing in something waterproof.

Wearing capris in the rain could mean damp ankles.

Madison headed back to the closet, picking

through the other clothes that were hanging and piled up in there, including some loose brown cotton pants, a blue skirt with embroidered pockets, and a pair of patched jeans. After many unsuccessful try-ons, Madison decided that the capris were really the best after all. She tugged them back on, donned a dark green T-shirt, slid on her sneakers and some little ankle socks with brown trim, and pulled her hair into a French twist just like the one she'd seen some star wear to a movie premiere. It looked a lot like the way her favorite teacher, Mrs. Wing, wore her hair, too.

"Well, isn't that a fancy hairdo for a cloudy day," Mom said. She'd been standing at Madison's bedroom door.

"How long have you been there?" Madison laughed.

"Long enough to see you're having a fashion emergency."

"Do I look okay?" Madison asked.

"Well, your hair is great, but don't you think your outfit looks a little . . . well, drab. . . . A bit like you're going into the army or something . . ."

"The army? Mom, it's camouflage. It's supposed to be cool."

"If you say so," Mom conceded.

"Mo-o-o-o-om! Don't tease me!" Madison wailed. She picked up one of the fluffy purple pillows from her bed and hurled it toward Mom.

"Hey," Mom cried out, catching the pillow. "Whatever you decide to wear, honey bear, you need to shake a leg. We don't want to be late."

Since the kids from all classes needed to be lined up in front of the building for the buses to Lake Dora no later than eight thirty, Madison had decided to forgo the usual walk to school. Mom would be chauffeur for the morning.

"Do you have your bathing suit?" Mom asked Madison on her way out the door.

"Yup," Madison said as she pulled up her T-shirt. "I put it on first. This way I don't have to change clothes in front of the whole class. I hate that. Not that we'll be doing much lake swimming if it rains . . ."

"Well, hurry up with whatever else you have to do," Mom said, turning to go. "I'll be downstairs."

Madison took one last look in the mirror and then followed. Since the rush was on, Mom had packed up a cold orange (already peeled) and a fruit-and-nut granola bar for Madison to eat on the ride to school. Madison stuffed it into her bag and kissed Phinnie good-bye.

By the time the two of them arrived in front of FHJH, most of the seventh-grade kids were already waiting there in groups. No one had really lined up yet. Madison gave Mom a peck on the cheek and hopped out of the car.

"Hello!" Madison called out to Madhur and Fiona as she walked over to join them. Aimee and Lindsay came over a moment later.

"Hiya, bus buddy!" Aimee cried, tapping Madison on the shoulder.

"Bus buddy? Cool!" Fiona said. Then she tapped Lindsay.

Jokingly, Madhur looked around and then tapped herself. "I guess I'll just be my own bus buddy," she declared proudly. The five girls laughed.

The only difficulty with a fivesome was the fact that they weren't an even number. Pairing off always left someone out. Usually, the five of them traded off on being the "solo" person, but most of the time, Madhur was odd girl out. Not that it mattered to her. Madhur survived as well on her own as she did in a crowd. That was a quality Madison envied.

The teachers divided the bus lines up by home-room at first, but then everyone screamed and moaned and complained. In the end, the kids got their way, arguing that friends should be able to sit with one another, since it was the end of the year. With "free seating" in place, Hart, Egg, Chet, Drew, and Dan lined up directly behind the girls. That was good news for everyone, especially Madhur. Now there were ten friends together: an even number. And Madhur didn't have to worry about not having a bus buddy. Chet immediately slipped into the seat next to her. The rest stayed seated in their own pairs.

"As you can all see, it looks like rain," said Mr.

Gibbons from the front of the bus. He was one of the teacher chaperones for the trip that day. Like the other teachers, he was dressed ultracasually, in jeans and a T-shirt emblazoned with the FHJH logo.

"Mr. Gibbons is cute in regular clothes," Aimee whispered to Madison, who promptly laughed out loud.

"Are you *kidding*?" Madison cried, incredulous.

"No," Aimee said seriously. Then she cracked a smile. "Okay, maybe he doesn't look *that* cute. I was just saying . . ."

"Shhhh! We can all hear you, and you sound *stupid*!" someone whispered from a row ahead.

Of course, Madison knew who it was. Who else but Ivy knew so well how to poke her nose . . . or in this case, her *ears* . . . into every situation? Ivy was good at hearing everything, except important information in science class.

Madison glared up ahead at her nemesis, but Poison Ivy didn't turn around.

"Beast," Aimee whispered under her breath.

Madison laughed softly, hoping that Ivy had heard *that* at least.

"So!" Mr. Gibbons said, clapping his hands. "Shall we sing a song?"

A couple of kids at the very back of the bus groaned, but almost everyone else cheered. And so, for the next twenty minutes or so, most of the kids sang along with Mr. Gibbons.

The ride to Lake Dora was as bumpy as ever. Madison found herself staring at the back of Hart's neck, wishing that she were in the seat next to him. Strangely, he didn't turn around once.

"What's up with Hart? He's being so quiet." Aimee whispered to Madison at one point. "Does he know about the whole Will thing?"

Madison's heart sank. "No, of course not!" she cried defensively. Then she thought for a moment. "At least, I don't think he knows."

"See? Fiona and I told you . . ." Aimee said.

"Told me *what*?" Madison snapped. Aimee's comments were beginning to annoy her.

For some reason, a vague memory from fifth grade popped into Madison's head. She recalled catching a sunfish with Hart at another lake, Lake Wannalotta. There was a photograph of that proud moment somewhere. Was it at Hart's place? Or was it back at her house? Why couldn't Madison remember? For so many years, they'd danced around the idea of liking each other. Now that it was all out in the open, could it last? Could Madison make it last? She needed to be Hart's girlfriend that summer and in the eighth grade. And in ninth grade after that. And then in high school, too, and maybe even college. This was one of those relationships that lasted forever, wasn't it? Wasn't that how it always worked in books and on TV shows?

Madison heard Gramma Helen's voice inside

129

her head. *Good things come to those who wait.*

Madison would just have to wait to see how everything turned out.

"Can you believe this is our last field trip?" Fiona asked.

"This year, you mean," Lindsay said.

"Yeah," Fiona said. "But it feels like the end of something else, doesn't it?"

Madison shrugged. All that overthinking (again) about Hart had put her in a sour mood. She didn't want this trip—or any trip—to be the end of anything.

By the time the buses arrived at Lake Dora, the sky was beginning to clear. Madison hoped that that was a positive sign. Everyone disembarked and headed for the waterfront. The air was thick with humidity, probably due to the cloud cover. There was hardly any breeze, even close to the water.

Down by the lake's edge, some of the seventh graders sat on the sand, patiently waiting for the other groups to get there. A few camp instructors arranged themselves on the interconnected docks, waiting to assist anyone who wanted to swim or get on a boat. One kept blowing his whistle to keep the kids from dangling their toes in the water.

Mr. Gibbons and the other teachers did their best to chaperone as the kids raced around to check out the water sports that were available. There were kayaks, rowboats, and rafts. And there were group competitions scheduled to start about a half hour after everyone arrived.

Over a rusty bullhorn, Mr. Gibbons announced that the first event of the day would be the rowboat race.

That meant that everyone had to get into their bathing suits or risk getting wet clothes.

"Would the following students please step forward?" Mr. Gibbons called out. He read off some familiar names: P. J. Rigby, Beth Dunfey, Jason Szelewski, and Suresh Dhir. Then he called out some *really* familiar names: Walter Diaz, Drew Maxwell, Madhur Singh, Fiona Waters, Hart Jones, and— unbelievably—Ivy Daly.

Ivy Daly? No way!

This first wave of participants piled into rowboats. There were five boats, with two kids per boat. Teachers had assigned the partners. Madhur partnered with Beth in a faded green rowboat with one cracked oar. Egg and Fiona were put together in a red boat. (Madison couldn't believe they'd ended up together, the lucky ducks.) Then P.J. paired with Suresh, and Drew went with Jason.

That left Hart and Ivy—together!—in a blue boat.

Madison was the one feeling the real blues, though. She wanted to capsize that boat before letting Hart sail away with her enemy. How could the teachers have thought that Hart and Ivy made sense as boating partners?

Aimee thought it was karma.

"Of course they put those two together," she said, "for all those Will comments yesterday. I told you."

Madison punched Aimee in the shoulder when she said that; not hard enough to leave a bruise, but hard enough so Aimee knew Madison was upset.

"Ignore them. Let's cheer Fiona and Madhur on," Lindsay said.

"Yes, let's," Madison said.

Who was Madison kidding though. She couldn't ignore them. The only rowboat racer she kept in her sights was Hart. Why were he and Ivy sitting so close together? Why was Hart smiling? And what was Ivy talking about nonstop?

She was probably batting those eyelashes and flipping that hair. And even though Hart said he thought she was a loser, Madison knew that Ivy had ways of making things happen.

The teachers blew their whistles. The race was on. The water on the lake started to get choppy as the kids rowed as fast as they could away from the shore and docks, out to a minicourse with buoys that had been set up a few yards away. Up above the lake, a trio of gulls circled around.

Beth and Madhur's boat looked as if it were going to tip over, but it stayed on an even keel.

Everyone wore beat-up life jackets from the boathouse, just in case of an accident.

"Go, Fiona! Go, Madhur!" Aimee cheered very loudly.

Madison and Lindsay joined in. "Go! Go! Go!"

Nearby, Madison heard Ivy's drones cheering, too. "Go, Ivy! Go, Hart!"

Hart?

Madison shot them a look. How dare they cheer on Hart—*her* Hart?

In the end, it was Drew and Jason who got back to the docks first and won the big prize, which consisted of two red ribbons that said YOU'RE THE TOPS! along the side.

"That's so cheesy," Madison commented to Aimee.

It was time for Madison to get ready. She had to peel off her fatigues, down to her bathing suit. The changing rooms at Lake Dora were crowded and had wet sand on the floor. Fortunately she was able to change quickly.

After the first and second races, Madison hoped to talk to Hart, just to find out what had happened out there on the lake, but she couldn't find him right away. When the third wave of boat riders moved in, her name was finally called, and she was paired up with some kid she hardly knew from her math class named David Smart. But she wasn't totally stranded. Lindsay was in the same group of rowers, and she kept making weird hand signals to Madison from

133

her place a few boats over. Madison was grateful for the distraction.

Her mood changed for the better when she and David started rowing. Before she knew it, they had raced around their buoys, pulled up to the docks, and won the first prize in their group.

When Madison stepped out of her rowboat, David's friends rushed over with high fives for him. Madison's pals did the same. That was when she came face to face with Hart again.

"Nice rowing, Finnster," Hart said. Madison tried hard to act cool, but she melted at the compliment. Besides, he looked adorable standing there in his damp T, palm-tree-print swim shorts, and backward-facing baseball cap.

From that moment on, it was as if nothing bad or strange or tense had ever happened between the two of them. Hart seemed as attentive as ever.

Aimee noticed the change. "I guess your boyfriend's back," she said.

Madison made a face.

Once again, the usual guy and girl friends clustered together for games of volleyball and horseshoes, and for lunch on the picnic tables. There was a momentary scare when Fiona, who was allergic to bee stings, was almost stung by one, but they all kept their cool. The day was hazy and lazy, and there were no more surprises; not even from Ivy or her drones. During lunch, teachers patrolled the picnic area, offering kids cold bottles of water and juice boxes. Despite being dressed in their casuals, the teachers were as officious as ever, wanting the kids to stay properly hydrated.

At the various picnic tables, the topics of conversation were the same: how to feel about the end of school and how to deal with next year. At Madison's table, Drew started talking up his big end-of-the-year bash, a blow-out party to be held in his backyard. Drew's parties were always the biggest, loudest, and most expensive. In fact, they'd started seventh grade with a Drew Maxwell party. It hardly seemed possible that they'd reached the end of the year already—and would soon be headed back to his house for yet another bash.

Suddenly, a burst of extraloud thunder interrupted their lunch. Everyone looked up just in time to see (and feel) big, fat raindrops. Egg opened his mouth to drink some; then everyone else followed suit and stuck out their tongues to taste the rain. Madison laughed at the sight of her classmates and friends sitting there at the Lake Dora waterfront, heads thrown back, tongues out.

Mr. Gibbons ruined the picture-perfect moment with a whistle. "Everyone!" he cried. "No messing around! Let's head indoors! Hurry! This looks like a bad storm."

Teachers rallied around the picnic tables to collect the kids and their lunches, making certain no

135

garbage was left behind in the downpour. Everyone had to grab their clothing, too, before it got too wet. Many of the boys had on their swimsuits instead of shorts, so they raced for the changing rooms. The girls grabbed their T-shirts and sun-dresses and did the same.

"Some field trip," one kid grumbled as he dashed across a lawn in front of Madison. "This bites."

Madison leaned back and stuck out her tongue again. She disagreed. The rain tasted cool, and she didn't mind it one bit.

The changing rooms were crammed, and the air felt heavy and humid with everyone crowding in. Lake Dora's rowboats weren't the only things in need of repairs, Madison noticed. Several toilets were marked "Out of Order," and one sink had no running water. But something about the broken-down state of things seemed right. Life, school, and even Lake Dora were imperfect things. And it was okay to be imperfect.

The bus ride home in the pouring rain felt like something out of a movie, with the wind blowing hard outside and darkness moving in even though it was still the middle of the day. Madison and her friends had planned to spend most of the return bus ride playing Truth or Dare, but instead they stared out the wet windows, entranced by the weather.

"Hey, kids," Mr. Gibbons called out from the front of the bus. "Driver Joe tells me that the weather forecast is for rain until tonight and into tomorrow. So, we're headed back to the school building for regular dismissal. Since we have about an hour before the school buses and your parents arrive to pick you up, we will unload the buses and have you go directly to your homerooms. Your homeroom teachers will have a snack and activities waiting for you there."

Kids on the bus booed softly. No one wanted to go back into the school building on a field-trip day. Madison, however, didn't mind; she was having dinner that night with Dad and Stephanie, and getting home early would give her more time to get ready and do homework—namely, the science project.

The bus lurched over the bumps in the road, and the kids screamed and wailed loudly, playing up the drama of the storm outside with a storm of their own inside the bus.

"Hey, look at that!" Madhur cried out, pointing outside the window to the banks of a river alongside the road. There, the water was rising fast. Parts of the road were beginning to flood.

Madison imagined their bus sliding off the road, taking a deep dive into the water, and floating away on the stormy current. She glanced around at her friends and classmates and at the teachers in the seats around her. She imagined them floating away, too. And then she thought about something Mr. Gibbons had said in English class way back at the start of the year: *expect the unexpected.*

Madison was always making and remaking plans for what she wanted at the end of seventh grade: a comfy relationship with Hart; good grades; a truce with Ivy; and so on. But perhaps it was better to look for the great un-expectations that were headed her way, rather than anticipating all the sure things. There were still enormous surprises to be had in the final weeks of school, like possible car accidents by the side of the road; rising, raging rivers; and even secret crushes.

All Madison could really do was hold her breath, brace herself, and go with the flow.

Chapter 12

A window in Madison's bedroom had been left slightly open during the rain-filled day. Now it was nearly nine thirty at night, and the air inside felt damp and cool for June.

Phin curled up by Madison's feet, purring more like a feline creature than a canine one. But he always purred whenever he sensed that there was something wrong with Madison. It was a comforting noise; it was his way of saying, "There, there, it'll be okay."

Madison needed a little reassurance. She could never have been prepared for the day—and night— she had had. From the trip, to the way dinner with Dad went afterward, everything had been unexpected.

Dinner was over now and Madison was online. She opened a late-day e-mail from Bigwheels. There was an attachment at the bottom: a poem. It had been a while since Bigwheels had sent one of those. Madison read over the text once, twice, and a third time. The corners of her mouth turned up in a crescent-shaped grin.

For MadFinn

My keypal, you
Always make me smile,
Delivering e-mail day and night.
If I need a shout-out, you're there
Saying the right thing
Online and never (ever) forgetting me.
Nothing can compare to us,
Fast friends across the miles,
In good mail and bad.
No one gets me like you do,
Now and (friends) forever,
Yours till the Web sites.

Madison quickly clicked COPY. Then she opened a new file, hit PASTE, and saved the poem as its own document. As she reread the words a fourth time, Madison noticed something extraspecial about the poem. The first letters of each line going down spelled something out: it was her name, Madison Finn, except for the Y at the end. But she didn't mind being Madison Finny for one poem.

After hitting SAVE, Madison began to type some text of her own. No poems here, though. Instead, Madison reported about dinner.

 Moving On (and On)

Rude Awakening: I've heard of the nuclear family, but this is ridiculous. Dad and Stephanie sure know how to drop a bomb.

Tonight at dinner I was blabbing on (and on) about the Hart-boat-race/jealous-of-Ivy moment. I had to fess up about Will, too, which was sort of embarrassing. And then KERBLAM! Dad butts in about how he and Stephanie have this big--no HUMONGOUS--news.

Of course, I imagine the worst thing right away, like the Big D Revisited. Stephanie laughed and said, "oh no" and got all lovey-dovey with Dad. It was kind of gross. She kissed his ear. My next thought was, "You're having a BABY!?" She laughed again and said something like, "Not yet." I was relieved. I mean, one day I'd like a brother or sister (I guess) but not now.

Dad finally spilled the beans. "We're moving, Maddie," he said. My whole stomach flops. Where? I feel like shrieking right there in the middle of Tamales Mexican restaurant. Instead, I stuff three nachos into my mouth.

Dad says they decided to sell the apartment in downtown Far Hills and build a

house, a big, suburban, house in some
development. Here are the facts:

1. They are building a 4,000-square-foot
   house with central air-conditioning
   and a central vacuum cleaner
   (whatever that is) AND a library.
   That makes the new house *twice* the
   size of the house we live in now.
2. They will build the house on this big
   tract of land so they'd have a giant
   yard where Phinnie can come and run
   around to play and maybe they'll even
   get another dog--or two--and Phinnie
   would get a brother or sister pooch.
   Maybe that'll be like practice for
   when they decide to have a real baby?
3. They will only be a 15- or 20-minute
   drive from the house on Blueberry
   Street. So nothing will change in
   terms of weekly dinners.

As Dad talked, I inhaled this slice of
mocha cake. That helped a lot. Sugar to the
rescue again.

Does getting a huge suburban home mean
Dad wants me to spend more time at his
house than the one I live in now? What will
that mean for me and Mom?

While she was typing, Madison's eyes drooped.
She lifted her head and tried to write more, but it
was no use. This day was over and out. If she was
going to survive the rest of the week's revue

run-throughs, test preps, and science experiments, she needed rest.

Phin obviously agreed.

He was already snoring.

After a good night's snooze, Thursday started with a bang, literally. Mom was about to drive Madison to school when the car backfired—*BOOM*—in the driveway. It sent shock waves through Phinnie, who was prancing around in the backseat. He dived to the floor with a yelp.

"Sorry about that," Mom croaked as she put the car in reverse and then first gear. "Is Phin okay?"

Madison spun around and checked. The poor dog was shaking *and* shedding.

"He's a wreck, of course," Madison said. She gently scratched Phin's head.

Madison wished that someone would scratch *her* head, too, and tell *her* everything would be okay.

Later in the day, when Madison strolled into Mrs. Wing's computer lab for her midafternoon class, Egg was perched by his usual monitor, chatting with Drew and another kid, Lance. He looked up right away when he saw Madison.

"Hey, Maddie," Egg called out. "What's wrong?" He had a look of genuine concern on his face.

Madison frowned. Since when did Egg notice her mood in the middle of school?

"Nothing's wrong," Madison replied, a little wary of his question.

"Nothing's wrong . . . except for your hair!" Egg joked.

Madison had to smile at his comment. In that moment, a bad joke seemed to work just as well as a kind word.

"You do all the inputs for Mrs. Wing, right?" Lance asked Madison. "We just got a new pile today."

"Yeah, she left some more for you on your desk," Drew said.

"Oh," Madison said.

She checked her cubicle and saw the short stack of papers. More inputting of seventh-grade data and memory pages wasn't such a bad thing, however. It meant Madison could focus on the computer and not on the boys.

Madison poked away at the keypad, entering names and statistics for each student page in her pile. Later, the students would scan in class photos to add to the memory pages. As Madison read through the text in front of her, she was reminded of the fact that she had not yet considered her own profile for the site.

Mrs. Wing came around to everyone's desks, as usual. She shooed Lance back to his own seat and crouched down in front of Madison's chair.

"How are you doing?" Mrs. Wing asked.

Madison shrugged. "Okay, I guess," she said.

"Overwhelmed? Excited? Feeling older?" Mrs. Wing inquired. "I can't believe it's been a whole year. Can you?"

Madison just shrugged again, silently. "I guess."

"Moving up from seventh grade is a big deal!" Mrs. Wing declared.

"Yeah," Madison said. "Bigger than big, actually."

"You know," Mrs. Wing whispered, "I've been meaning to tell you how much I have enjoyed having you in my class and on the Web site team. I've always felt a strong connection between us. I am lucky to have so many gifted students."

"Really? I'm one of those?"

"Of course," Mrs. Wing said. As she draped her arm around Madison's shoulder and the back of the chair, Mrs. Wing's bracelets jangled. It was her trademark sound. Madison knew she would miss that and everything else about her favorite seventh-grade teacher.

Jangle, jangle.

"Thanks for being so helpful," Madison said meekly, wanting to pay Mrs. Wing some compliments of her own.

"Of course," Mrs. Wing winked. Still jangling, she walked on to the next student. In a way, Mrs. Wing's bracelets had the same sort of calming effect on Madison as a head-scratch had on Phinnie.

After computer class, and then social studies

class, Thursday ended with the opposite of a bang. Madison looked all over for Aimee or Fiona to walk home with her. But Fiona was apparently playing soccer, and Aimee had disappeared. Madison flipped open her cell phone and called Mom at work. She decided she wanted to head over to the animal clinic with Dan and needed permission.

Dan was psyched to have Madison join him. With all the work at school (and out of school), she had not been around to volunteer as much as she had in the fall. Together, they took the bus ride across town, where Dan's mother, Eileen, met them.

Dan and Madison worked for a while in the back room of the clinic, cleaning cages and doing the late-afternoon feedings. A crate of new puppies, along with their mother, had come in to the clinic just that morning—the abandoned mommy German shepherd had been reported giving birth in an alley. The pups needed baths, standard shots, and, of course, clinic names. Every new animal that arrived at the clinic got a real name, not just a number, like Pekingese 2 or Manx 3 or Parrot 4. It was Dan's job, with Madison's help, to assist Dr. Wing and his staff with the bathing and shots, but it was the naming process that got them most excited.

"Isn't it crazy that you've been volunteering here for a whole year now?" Dan said as they brainstormed to come up with cute names for the fluffy pups.

146

"It doesn't feel like a year," Madison said. "But what is a year supposed to feel like?"

"Huh?" Dan asked, looking quizzically at Madison.

"A year? What is it supposed to feel like? Oh, never mind," Madison said, looking away. "We have to name the puppies. Come on!"

"Uh . . . what about Doggy Doo One and Two?" Dan said, laughing a little.

"*So* not funny," Madison groaned.

"Dog Wonder?"

"Lame."

"Hey, it's not like you're dishing out any bright ideas. What about *Madison*? That's a good dog name."

"Oh, aren't you real cute?" Madison said, giving Dan a quick shove.

Dan fell back and cried out as if in pain, when of course he wasn't in any pain at all. Breaking into laughter, he sounded like some kind of deranged cartoon character.

Watching him stand there, fake-wincing and laughing through his nose, Madison's mind began to go into rewind mode. She remembered another day that year, when she had discovered that he'd been her secret admirer.

For some reason, as she thought about Dan and the past and boys in general, the name Will came into her head like a kernel of corn in a hot pan—*POP*. Madison chased it away as quickly as it had come in and tried to think about something else. Something *nonboy*.

Back home, later that night, Madison watched a little TV with Phinnie and Mom. They spent a lot of time discussing Dad's big news about the house. Mom was all thumbs-up and smiles about the move, despite Madison's misgivings.

While they sat there, the phone rang. Mom grabbed the receiver. It was a Budge Films executive, calling later than late. Mom sat there listening on the portable, chatting about the Japan film project with her boss. Suddenly, Madison noticed, Mom paused to take another call; the line must have beeped.

"Oh, dear," Mom said into the phone. "I'm sorry, but I'm on the line with an important call right now. Can I have Maddie call you back?"

Madison glanced over at the phone and at Mom's face and mouthed the words *Who is it?* as clearly as she could.

It was probably Hart.

Mom waved Madison off, unable to tell her, and grabbed a pen from the table. She scribbled some words on the back of a magazine. When she switched off that call and returned to her work call, a grinning Mom pushed the magazine in front of Madison and covered the receiver for a split second.

"Were you expecting him to call?" Mom asked softly. The note read: WILL CALLED.

Madison's mouth dropped open. Will? He had her e-mail *and* her phone number? He was trying to get in touch *again*? Her heart skipped a beat, as she thought about him, somewhere in the middle of New York City, trying to get in touch. Here she was, in the middle of Far Hills, with no clue as to how to respond.

She needed a clue.

Clicking off the TV, and leaving Mom and the dog alone in the living room, Madison raced upstairs to her laptop. She quickly logged on to bigfishbowl.com and briefly considered Ask the Blowfish as an option. After all, as had happened so many times before, Madison could simply ask, "What do I do?" and the Blowfish would give her the best advice in the world.

Or not.

Rather than rely upon a computerized fish for help with major life decisions, Madison decided to rely on her own wisdom (or lack thereof). She began to write, composing a real reply to Will's notes—and calls. It was about time. Her scribbles gradually took the form of scientific equations. It seemed as if everything were finally getting in sync, at least a little bit.

<u>What is your scientific goal?</u> To like someone for real.
<u>What is the scientific question you</u>

are trying to answer? Do I "like-like" or just "like" Will? Why do I want to talk to him so much even though I can't write him one lousy e-mail? Or, am I a terrible person for liking someone other than Hart?

<u>Give a detailed explanation of how you will conduct the experiment to test your hypothesis.</u> I will e-mail Will back <u>finally</u> and say hello. Then I will see what he says after that, crossing my fingers and holding my breath. In the meantime, I will tell Hart nothing.

<u>Keep a detailed journal of data measurements.</u> Details to come.

Madison leaned back.

It suddenly seemed that everything in seventh grade boiled down to science.

Madison had a lot to learn.

Chapter 13

 The Looooooong Weekend

I can't believe the weekend is over already.

Friday was total fuzz. In the hallway, Ivy made some crack to me about how she'd done NO work (yes, nothing, *nada*, zip) on our Blue Sky project and I came this close to slugging her lights out. And I'm not even a violent person. LOL!!! Of course I spent most of Friday morning and afternoon still obsessing about Will. I tried to write something back after his second e-mail (yes, he sent another one) and his phone call (eeeps!), but every single word

I wrote sounded moronic, so I did a major DELETE.

All in all, parts of the weekend were generally boring, which is not what I expected. I figured we'd all be hanging out before the end of school, having parties and sleepovers, but life was pretty much the same as usual. Mom had me help her clean the house (just call me "vacuum and dusting girl," ok?). She's starting to panic about not having enough time to juggle her new job and the big moving-up party she's having for me and the rest of our family. Mom is so bad at hiding stress. But I am very glad that she didn't take that other, harder job, for sure. She would have a meltdown every other day with THAT stress.

Somehow this weekend I did manage to make time on Sunday for homework (thanks to Mom's endless nagging) and despite my lame partner, I worked up a great outline for our science project. I copied a BUNCH of stuff into the notebook. Not only that, but I found these 2 awesome experiments that we can use to PROVE our theories. Woo-hoo. Mr. Danehy will be so proud. Well, as proud as he gets. One experiment shows how light is refracted. We have to use nail polish, too, for the test (Ivy should LOVE that part). The other experiment has to do with shining light through soapy water. I'm not totally sure how that works, but it should be impressive. I want to be impressive PLUS.

Didn't some famous scientist say that for every action there is an equal and opposite reaction? I've decided that for every enemy action, I'll provide an equal and opposite reaction. That translates into Ivy = bad & Maddie = good.

Rude Awakening: Bigwig scientists aren't the only ones who have something to prove. I have something to prove, too.

Madison hit SAVE. She was killing time on Monday morning before science class, up in the library at school. Mr. Books, the librarian, lurked nearby, as usual. He was always ready to seize the moment if someone talked too loudly or stayed on the computer longer than his or her allotted time.

There were other kids there in the library doing the same thing as Madison. All year long she'd been going up there to work, think, and escape. It was probably her favorite place in the entire junior high school building, despite Mr. Books's funny looks.

Today, Madison opted to use one of the library computers rather than her laptop. While sitting at the terminal, she heard a low, humming sound coming from her orange bag. Her cell phone was vibrating. The telltale outline of an envelope lit up right away in the corner of the phone display. There was a text message.

Although Madison had gotten her cell phone a

while ago, she was still adjusting to its ring tones, vibrations, and hidden message indicators.

Hey, where r u? Gesswat? Im switching back 2 props for the revue ok b/c I promised ok?? IM me
Hart

Madison text-messaged him right back.

Thx ((U))
TTYL
Maddie

Madison jumped up from the computer where she'd been sitting and typing. Hart was back on her team!

She happily wandered away from her purple notebook and the other books on the table so she could search the library shelves for a novel. Mr. Gibbons had requested one more book report for the school year, and he had given permission to the class to read *anything*.

She scanned the shelves for at least ten minutes, stopping to glance here and there at books with interesting titles or covers. Being there reminded her of times when she'd been there with her BFFs, laughing about someone's dumb crush or cramming for a test.

There really would be nothing like seventh grade ever again.

"What are you doing? Don't we have science class?" Ivy Daly said, appearing suddenly from around the side of one of the bookcases.

Madison groaned. It was bad enough that she had to see the enemy in science class—but *before* science class, too?

"I'm looking for a book," Madison said curtly.

"Duh, we're in a library. I could have guessed that much," Ivy said. "You want to walk to class together?"

"Together?" Madison asked. "Um . . ."

What else was she supposed to say?

"Sure, I guess," Madison mumbled.

Ivy looked pleased with herself. Madison wasn't quite sure why.

Madison picked up her books, and they walked down to Mr. Danehy's classroom.

"We have to present our outline today," Ivy whispered to Madison.

Madison looked at her dumbly. "Uh . . . *yeah* . . . I know."

"Well, I was just making sure you did know, because we want to make a good impression, right?" Ivy said.

"Right," Madison said as they entered the room.

"Welcome to P-Day, students," Mr. Danehy said, his voice booming even louder than usual.

"P-Day?" Chet asked from the other side of the room.

Madison giggled.

"Project Day, Mr. Waters. And since you were our first to speak today, then go ahead and start us off. How is your project coming along? You and Mr. Jones have something to share, yes?"

Madison eyed Hart from her seat. She nodded sweetly, and he nodded back. They were speaking without words. What she was saying silently was, *I feel so guilty that I was thinking about Will, but I really do like you, Hart, I really*, really *do.*

This time, she hoped he could read minds.

Mr. Danehy was pleased with Hart and Chet's experiment and project outline. They called their assignment "A Couple of Fungis."

Chet said it at least four times, stressing the bad joke. "A couple of fun guys? Get it? Get it?"

"Oh, yes, Mr. Waters, we get it," Mr. Danehy sighed. Then he turned to the next pair of students for their outline presentation. All of the kids so far had their assignments in order, and Madison was beginning to wonder if she and Ivy could pull it off, too. She knew that she had done the right research and that she had the factual information to back up her claims, but would she be able to make it seem as though she and Ivy worked together? It wouldn't be an easy task.

She shouldn't have worried. When Mr. Danehy finally turned to Madison and Ivy, it was Ivy who spoke first. That surprised Madison. But what Ivy *said* shocked Madison even more.

"Well," Ivy chirped, in that superior, know-it-all voice that she put on sometimes, "we did a lot of digging to find just the right tests to prove that the sky is, indeed, blue. One experiement, using soap, water, and a flashlight, will show that . . ."

Madison glared at Ivy when she started to explain the particulars of the experiment. How could she possibly have done the same research as Madison? How could she possibly have reached such similar conclusions? Since when did Ivy surf the Net as well as Madison?

"For experiment number two," Ivy continued, "We'll talk about light refraction using a safety pin, water, black paper, and nail polish. . . ." She flashed her own polished nails.

What was going on?

"We learned in class this year that visible light is the part of the electromagnetic spectrum that our eyes can see. . . ."

Madison was ready to jump up and shout, "Say what?" Ivy couldn't have read the chapters on that subject, could she? She hadn't even been able to pronounce the word "electromagnetic" five minutes ago, and she certainly couldn't *spell* it.

This was fraud, pure and simple. But before Madison could say anything to dispute—or, for that matter, add to—her partner's contribution, Mr. Danehy spoke right up.

"My goodness, what a turn of events!" he cried.

Ivy nodded and grinned. She looked over at Madison with a self-satisfied sneer; only, no one else but Madison could see that from any other angle but her own.

"I'm astonished, Ms. Daly," Mr. Danehy went on. "Simply astonished. You've certainly done your homework. Ms. Finn, I'd say you have quite a partner here. I'd like to hear about some of your contributions to this fine presentation."

Madison started to speak—*wanted* to speak—but the words wouldn't come out. They were like molasses on her tongue, thick and stuck.

"Ms. Finn?" Mr. Danehy asked a second time. He crossed his arms as he always did when he was starting to get impatient.

"I . . . I . . ." Madison stammered. "I have a whole outline here of facts about rays, I mean, Rayleigh scattering . . . I think . . ."

She searched in her notebook for the right notes, but they didn't turn up right away.

"I don't have all day," Mr. Danehy moaned. "Rayleigh scattering is very good. What else do you have?"

That was when Ivy began speaking again.

"Well!" Ivy piped up. "It all has to do with variables in the earth's atmosphere. Here on Earth, the sun appears yellow, but if you looked at it from space, it would actually appear white. . . ."

Madison wanted to interrupt with a raised finger

just to say, "Okay, so you're saying all this, Ivy, but what does it *mean*? As if you know!"

Ivy continued, eyes twinkling. Madison was *this* close to throwing up.

She caught Hart's eye again. He was frowning, but when Madison made eye contact, he smiled a little bit. It was some comfort, considering the fact that the rest of Madison's universe was on the verge of collapse.

Mr. Danehy stood back, arms now uncrossed, still shaking his head in a combination of disbelief and pride.

"The first steps toward correctly explaining the color of the sky were taken by John Tynder . . . I mean, *Tyndall* . . ." Ivy said, elaborating on another of the points about which Madison had written copious notes in her purple notebook.

That was when it dawned on Madison: Ivy was saying all the stuff Madison had researched. Ivy was practically *reciting* from Madison's notebook.

Madison's brain zipped back to the moment an hour before in the library, when Ivy had mysteriously appeared from nowhere in the stacks, saying that she'd been "looking for" Madison. How long had Madison been away from her notes at that point? That had been an ideal opportunity for idea theft. Could Ivy have done it that quickly? It didn't seem possible. Was she *that* good a thief?

Madison glared at Ivy, trying to make her squirm.

But Ivy was unflappable. Then Madison spotted a clue to Ivy's sudden genius. Under the lab table, Ivy clutched a white page—a copied page? Wait! The handwriting on the page was *Madison*'s. . . .

"You rat," Madison muttered under her breath.

Ivy turned and sneered again. "Squeak, squeak," she said, flaunting the copied page, at Madison alone.

"I can't *wait* for your project," Mr. Danehy pronounced to both girls. "And now, let's move along to our next pair of scientists."

Madison's head throbbed. All that work she'd done was ruined. And even worse, this was only the preproject presentation. How could she expose the enemy before or during the real presentation? There was no way to do it without looking vengeful and angry; Mr. Danehy hated tattlers. But he hated cheaters more, didn't he? Mr. Danehy had been on Ivy's case all year long, and now she was lying her way through Science.

What a mess.

If only Bigwheels were there right now to give Madison a dose of clever keypal wisdom.

Or maybe Gramma Helen. She always had something wise to say.

Then Madison remembered something very important: in just one hour, she'd be off to the airport with Mom to pick Gramma Helen up.

Gramma was coming! She'd know what to do. After all, she always did.

Brrrinnnggg!

The class bell rang, and Mr. Danehy threw his hands up in the air. Students who hadn't had a chance to present would have to do it during Mr. Danehy's study period that afternoon, or on the following day.

Ivy had a smug look on her face as she and Madison gathered up their books and headed for the classroom door. Madison joined Hart and Chet so that she wouldn't have to be around Ivy for another minute.

"You didn't tell me that Ivy actually studied," Hart blurted out as they walked into the hall.

"Ha!" Madison said. "As if. She stole all my work and passed it off as her own."

"No way," Chet said. Then he started to laugh. "Man, she's *good*."

"Chet," Hart groaned, "shut up."

Madison smiled when Hart rushed to her defense like that. In that moment, she let go of her paranoia about her feelings for Hart. Everything would be fine, Madison told herself.

I just have to believe in myself, she thought.

"Know what? You should tell the teacher what Ivy did," Chet said. "Don't let her get away with all that. . . ."

"Yeah," Hart agreed. "Mr. Danehy won't tolerate cheaters. In fact, didn't he say those exact words once?"

"I don't know," Madison shrugged. "There has to be a better way to give Ivy a taste of her own medicine. Can't I expose her without looking like a tattler?"

"You mean silent revenge?" Hart asked. "No way. You're too nice to do something mean."

"Not anymore!" Madison cried.

"Look out, Ivy," Chet said. "Madison Finn is out for blood!"

Hart chuckled, and the two boys walked a little bit ahead of Madison, trading a few more of their own jokes. Within moments, Madison had lost sight of both of them.

That was okay. She had other places to go. Namely, she had to meet the enemy so that they could review their final presentation strategy for Wednesday.

As another bell rang, Madison glanced at the digital readout on her cell phone to check the time. Oh, no! Madison had less than an hour before she had to meet Mom, who would probably be chomping at the bit to get to LaGuardia Airport to meet Gramma's plane.

Strangely, Ivy came on time to their designated meeting spot, looking as sly as ever. They were rendezvousing in a study hall on the first floor of the school. The room was practically empty, except for a few die-hard students.

"I can't believe you dared to show up!" Madison

declared right off the bat when she saw Ivy. "You're such a snake."

"Yeah, boo and hiss and all that," Ivy sneered. "Let's just figure out how we'll do the final presentation."

"Well, I think you should do it all," Madison said. "Since you were such a show-off today . . . with *my* notes."

"Don't be such a crybaby," Ivy said. "After all, we're both getting the same grade, aren't we? It's not like Mr. Danehy will give me an A and you a lower grade for the same project. Or maybe he will. . . ." Ivy started to snicker.

Madison pulled out her purple notebook and slammed it on the desk. "Let's just divide the topics. How about we open with a question like 'What is light?'"

"Fine," Ivy grunted. "You can do that. I'll do the nail polish experiment."

I knew it.

Madison sighed. "We need to make a poster or something that shows the color spectrum. I was thinking we could make a collage of different pieces of sky and clouds on a blue background. . . ."

"That sounds good. Why don't you do that, since you know what to do," Ivy suggested.

"Why don't I just do *everything*?" Madison cried.

"Fine with me," Ivy said. "Like I said, it's not like

we're getting a different grade or anything. That's the fun of being partners, right?"

Madison felt as though her head would explode. "Fine," she snapped. "I'll make the poster. I'm more creative than you anyhow."

"I wouldn't go *that* far," Ivy said. "You probably still use those Magic Markers that smell like fruit flavors."

"You know, Mr. Danehy will know you didn't really do the work," Madison said, ignoring Ivy's comment. "And if he doesn't figure it out, I'll tell him."

"Whatever," Ivy said. "Go ahead."

Madison couldn't believe that after everything that had happened between Ivy and her, it came down to this: a showdown between old friends-turned-enemies. Did Ivy know that Madison *wouldn't* tattle on her enemy?

"Why can't you just help and be nice . . . for once?" Madison pleaded.

Ivy smiled. "Why should I?"

Someone else in the study hall whispered a very loud *Shhhhh*, and so Madison and Ivy lowered their voices. It had become painfully clear to Madison that Ivy was not going to contribute in any significant way. Ivy probably knew that Madison wouldn't let the project dissolve, no matter who did what. She knew Madison would make the best collage and find the best examples to discuss. She knew she could ride Madison's hard work all the way to a better report card. It was what she'd been doing during Science all year.

Some things will never, ever change, Madison thought, whether they happen in third grade or seventh grade or any grade. Ivy will always be poisonous, as much as I want to give her a second (and third and fourth and so on) chance to be different.

Madison did convince Ivy to stay in the study hall with her for another twenty minutes, just to make sure they were clear about who would do the talking at what points in the presentation. But then, as soon as they'd worked their way down the list of information, Ivy grabbed her stuff and dashed off. Madison restuffed her orange bag and went out as well. Mom was probably waiting.

Sure enough, Mom's car was one of a few lingering parent vehicles lined up outside school. She stood outside the driver's-side door of the car, waiting for Madison to hop in.

Unfortunately, Madison and Mom hit all the traffic lights and stalled vehicles imaginable on the way to the airport. They couldn't catch a break at the toll lines either, where they waited for at least ten minutes to get through a cash lane. Mom had forgotten her E-ZPass.

"When your grandma gets here," Mom warned Madison as they drove on, "I want you to be on your best behavior."

"Aren't I always?" Madison asked.

Mom shot her a look. "Yeah," she said, smiling. "Usually."

"So what are you worried about?"

"Oh, I guess I'm thinking about Gramma being here, and then all of your dad's family being around the house, and I just don't want anyone to feel uncomfortable, and there's so much to do. . . ."

"This whole thing was *your* idea, Mom," Madison said. "Are you thinking about canceling it?"

"Cancel? Are you kidding?" Mom cried.

"Yeah, I guess we can't cancel. And since we can't, you should try to relax," Madison suggested.

"I know, I know," Mom said. "Oh, honey bear, I just hope this wasn't a bad idea."

"Mo-o-o-o-o-om!" Madison crooned. "It was a good idea. I'll help you get through the whole party, I swear. It'll be like old times."

"But things are so different now. Your dad has a whole new life. And your uncle Rick and your aunt Violet . . . I haven't seen them in over a year now."

Mom pulled off the main highway and followed the signs for United Airlines arrivals. Once the car was parked in short-term parking, Mom and Madison raced inside, up the escalator, and through a maze of concessions and shops toward the gates.

"Howdy-dooooo!" There was Gramma Helen, straw hat on her head, flowered scarf around her waist, standing with her rolling luggage in front of the security area. She waved as if she were flapping her wings.

"Gramma!" Madison howled when she saw her. She ran over and threw her arms out wide.

Gramma pretended to be winded by the hug. "Mercy!" she cried. "That's some kind of greeting! You'll squash me!"

"Hello, Mother," Mom said, leaning in for a kiss. They exchanged pleasant hellos and other small talk. Mom apologized for the traffic.

"I figured I'd wait right here at the X-ray station," Gramma said with a wink. "They won't let anyone through these metal detectors now. It's a shame you can't meet family right at the gate anymore."

"I have so much to tell you!" Madison said, jumping into the conversation.

"Well, I'm all ears—and I'm all yours," Gramma chuckled.

Gramma took Madison's hand in her own soft one, and they followed Mom back down the escalator to the parking lot.

Chapter 14

On Tuesday morning, Phin moped around the house.

Company wasn't the problem. He seemed thrilled that Gramma Helen was there. Since her arrival, he'd gotten one of her hand-knit sweaters (although it was really too hot to wear), a huge number of liver snaps and rawhide chews, and more kisses and back-scratches than he could have dreamed of.

What Phin wasn't too happy about was being left home alone while Madison, Mom, and Gramma Helen headed into New York City for a girl's day out: no dogs allowed.

Mom had written a special note to get Madison out of classes for that day. Although it meant Madison would miss a revue rehearsal and a possible pop quiz, she didn't mind. How could she? Days when she could bond with moms and grandmas didn't come along very often. Besides, she felt she could use a break from school and the craziness of the week before.

Mom decided it would be better to take the train in rather than risk the annoyance of rush-hour city traffic. The three of them had a quick cereal-and-OJ breakfast before heading down to the train station.

Sometimes things got tenser when Gramma Helen visited. Gramma and Mom would argue incessantly about household chores or politics or even Madison. Past visits had led to some feuds that had taken a day or more to get over. Madison typically felt trapped, forced to take sides. It was like the way Madison felt about the Big D between Mom and Dad, *and* the way she felt when her BFFs split ranks. Madison often ended up in the middle of things.

But today was different. Mom and Gramma were on their very best behavior, and Madison wasn't in the middle in a bad way at all. All morning long, Mom and Gramma both crowed about how proud they were to see Madison get through seventh grade with such good grades and good friends. And all that crowing gave Mom and Gramma a common bond. No arguing necessary.

The primary reason for the special day out in the big city was to purchase a new outfit for Moving Up Day. Mom had agreed to let Madison pick out a cool, new dress—*if* Mom came along on the shopping adventure. It seemed like a good plan to Madison. She got to spend quality time with Mom *and* get a groovy dress in the process. And having Gramma Helen along for the excursion made it that much better.

Boarding a morning train for New York during the workweek made Madison feel like some kind of executive, as if she were heading in for an important meeting or a business brunch. All around them she saw suit jackets and leather briefcases and people poking at their high-tech personal organizers. It was a world away from her FHJH homeroom.

The train ride to Grand Central terminal took only forty minutes. Madison loved the cool rush of the passengers moving out through the train doors, up the metal stairwells, and into the vast terminal. She, Mom, and Gramma quickly exited out onto Forty-second Street to grab a taxi. Mom wanted to show Gramma the new offices of Budge Films. They had just moved into a new space in Soho, in downtown Manhattan near Canal Street.

"We can check out the office and then head to Chinatown for lunch," Mom suggested.

"Oooh! Dim sum! Yum," Gramma cooed.

Madison laughed. "Fried rice and dumplings, please," she added. "I'm hungry already."

"I think there are some adorable boutiques near the new office," Mom said. "Maybe we'll find a sweet dress there. Otherwise, we can head back uptown to one of the department stores or maybe Madison Avenue."

"Madison Avenue!" Gramma said. "Now, that's perfection!"

Madison grinned, because of course she'd shopped there before, with Lindsay and all of her friends. Lindsay's aunt Mimi had taken them on a shopping spree for Lindsay's thirteenth-birthday party. And Madison had always thought there was something too good to be true about shopping on an avenue named after her.

"It all sounds like fun, Mom," Madison said as they climbed into a yellow taxi and rode over to Fifth Avenue.

They passed the New York Public Library, with its majestic lions perched out in front, and then moved downtown, past camera shops, restaurants, and loads of other taxicabs. Madison was stuck in the middle of the backseat between Gramma and Mom, on the hump, but she still had a good view out the window of the pedestrians. Some were tourists, with cameras dangling from their necks. Others held cell phones to their ears or adjusted their hands-free headsets. Everyone had somewhere to go and someone to talk to, even though most of the people were alone.

The taxi zoomed around a little green park at a part of the city called Union Square, where there was a vast dog park, people lying in the grass, and brightly colored paintings set out on display by various artists.

Just a few moments later, Mom said to the driver, "Stop over there," and they exited the cab. Madison clutched Gramma's hand as they walked across West Broadway toward Mercer Street. Mom turned into a brownstone building with a gargoyle staring down at them from over the enormous front door.

"What do you think?" Mom cried proudly. "Very cool place, right."

"Oh, Frannie, dear," Gramma said. "Everything you do impresses me."

"Mother," Mom said. "You're too much."

They entered a nondescript marble lobby that led to a large freight elevator. Several flights up, the elevator doors opened on to a sherbet-colored space filled with bright windows, plants, and geometric-patterned carpets. As they strolled inside, everyone said good morning to Mom, as though she were very important. Usually, Madison didn't get to see that "executive" side of Mom; and she liked it—a lot. It made *her* feel just as important.

Rounding a corner, Mom showed Madison and Gramma into her new office. A brass plaque on the lemon-colored door read: FRANCINE FINN, VICE PRESIDENT, PRODUCTION. From floor to ceiling, the room was stacked with papers and boxes of videocassettes and film. It looked a lot like Mom's office at home—only bigger.

On the bulletin board behind Mom's desk was a giant photograph of Madison and Phin taken at the beach the summer before. That caught Madison's attention.

"Wait. You have me hanging on your wall in my bathing suit?" Madison cried. "How mortifying."

"Oh, no," Mom smiled. "Look at how beautiful you two look. . . ."

"I look fat," Madison complained.

"Maddie!" Mom said. "Don't ever let me hear you say that. You look *beautiful*. You are beautiful."

"I agree one hundred percent," Gramma Helen said, squeezing Madison around the shoulders. "You shouldn't be so self-conscious, dear. Stop reading all those magazines."

"What magazines?" Madison asked.

"The ones with the skin-and-bones girls on the covers," Gramma Helen said, wagging her finger in Madison's face.

While they were standing there, Mom's assistant, Trey, came into the office. He carried a clipboard and a stopwatch and barely stopped to say hello on his way in or, later, out.

"Isn't this a lovely view?" Gramma Helen said, leaning toward the giant picture window behind Mom's messy desk. "I didn't think we were up very high, but you can see a lot from here."

Madison stared at the water towers, terraces, and building facades visible from Mom's office.

"Pure New York," Mom said. "I just love this new space. I'm so glad you helped me make up my mind to stay at Budge, Maddie."

"Hold on, Mom, I didn't do anything," Madison said.

"That's not what she told me!" Gramma Helen chirped.

Madison shrugged. "Well, I just want to see you more, Mom . . . and so does Phinnie, so I guess it made sense . . . to stay here. Besides, there's the trip to Japan to consider. . . ."

"Indeed," Mom added.

Everyone chuckled. A few moments later, they left mom's office and headed back to the elevator.

When they reached street level again, Madison took in as many of the sights and sounds of the area as she could: the smell of tar and garbage; the echo of bumper-to-bumper traffic on the side streets; the large canvases hanging in the windows of galleries, the small grocery stores, sometimes called bodegas, tucked in between the banks and the shoe stores. They had walked only a few blocks east when Madison happened to glance up at a large sign on a warehouse-type building located just across the street. It said, BROOME CONDOMINIUMS, INQUIRE INSIDE.

Madison racked her brain for a moment, trying to recall where she'd heard that name before.

"Mom, what streets are we near?" Madison asked.

174

Mom pointed up to the green street signs on the corner. They were standing at the intersection of Lafayette and Broome streets.

Madison's jaw dropped.

Now she remembered why the name sounded familiar.

This was Will's neighborhood. He'd talked about it at Camp Sunshine. He'd mentioned the street names and the art galleries and this condominium complex where he and his parents lived. He was a city boy, and *this* was his part of the city.

Holy cow.

Madison did a 180-degree turn where she was standing. Was Will somewhere nearby? Would she see him crossing the street here—or stepping into a delicatessen—or hailing a cab? Mom worked near Will's house! It seemed too coincidental to be believed, but it was true.

"Are you okay, honey bear?" Mom asked, gently taking Madison by the shoulder.

"Mom?" Madison looked up with wide eyes. "This is where Will lives."

"Who's Will?" Gramma Helen asked.

"Long story," Madison explained. "I told you about him once, when I was at that camp in Florida. Do you remember?"

Gramma laughed and shook her head. "Goodness' sakes, no! I can't keep track of all the boys in your life, dear."

"All the boys?" Madison said. "There aren't that many. What are you talking about?"

Gramma and Mom both chuckled at that, but Madison did not look amused. Part of her reaction came from the fact that Madison knew she had an acute case of boys on the brain lately.

As they walked on together, strolling in and out of a few dress shops that Mom knew about, Madison went into more detail about Will and camp and the e-mails and phone call. Gramma seemed keenly interested.

"Sounds like that boy likes you, dear," Gramma insisted. "A long-distance crush, eh?"

Madison kept shrugging it off. "No, not really," she said, even though deep inside she was thinking that very same thing.

They stopped in front of a clothing boutique called The Pink Elephant. Madison liked the name, but there weren't any dresses inside that were appropriate for the moving-up ceremony. Besides, everything seemed to be priced at $300 and up. As they strolled around, Madison kept her eyes open for signs of Will. She half-expected him to pop up from a brownstone stoop or jump out of a second-floor apartment window and yell, "Surprise! I knew it was you!"

Of course, that was all a zany daydream. What if Will didn't even live downtown anymore? It had been a while since camp. . . .

At that moment, Madison spotted a blond head across the street, standing by a street vendor. Her heart stopped, or at least it felt as though it had.

Could it be . . . ?

She couldn't make out the face, but her gut told her that maybe this really was him—the *real* him—the one she'd been thinking about ever since he had sent that e-mail. It had to be Will!

Madison started to breathe really hard.

"Maddie!" Mom said. "You sound like you're about to hyperventilate."

"Huh?"

The blond head was bobbing up and down. He was laughing. He was talking to another boy with black hair. They were buying hot dogs.

"Madison, dear," Gramma Helen said. "Your mother thinks we should keep looking for a dress for a while longer. . . ."

"I can't think about a dress!" Madison cried.

Where had he gone? There! At the corner. Why didn't he turn around?

"Maddie, what are you looking at?" Mom asked, glancing across the street at the same spot as Madison.

At that precise moment, the blond boy turned around to face them.

"Oh, no!" Madison let out a sad gasp.

"What is it?" Gramma Helen asked. Now the three of them stood on the curb, staring across the busy street at the hot-dog vendor.

Madison hung her head sadly as the boys walked away.

"What was *that* all about?" Mom asked.

"Nothing," Madison said. "Thought I saw someone I knew. That's pretty dumb, right?"

"Oh," Gramma said. "I always do that. Just the other day I thought I saw Grampa Joe in a crowd."

"You *did*?" Madison asked. Her grandfather had been dead for many years.

"Ah, yes," Gramma went on. "I think that's because I feel close to him. I feel like he's still right next to me, no matter what truly separates us. I see Joe in a lot of places."

"Really?" Madison asked.

"We should shake our tails, girls," Mom said, interrupting. "Let's finish this conversation at lunch."

Madison and Gramma each took the other's arm and walked closely together. Mom linked arms on Madison's opposite side. The three of them walked down the sidewalk as if they were attached at the hips. The family resemblance was obvious: hair, eyes, and high cheekbones. It would have been a picture-perfect photo, if anyone had had a camera.

As they walked on, Madison turned back once to see if she could catch a glimpse of the blond boy, or any other boy that looked like Will. It was impossible to let go of the hope that she might see him.

On the fringes of Chinatown, Mom led Madison

and Gramma Helen into another small boutique. By now, Madison's feet—and spirits—were tiring out. She was convinced that her ultimate dress was nowhere to be found—at least not in this neighborhood. But then, there it was! Madison smiled when she saw the purple sundress hanging by the front door: linen with lace and embroidered flowers around the hem. Little pearl buttons went up the back, and there was a grosgrain ribbon waist. Best of all, it fit Madison perfectly.

"I never would have picked out a purple dress," Madison said as she stared back at her reflection in the store mirror. "But I love, love, *love* this."

"Me, too," said Gramma.

"Yeah, it's just grape . . . I mean, *great*," Mom joked.

"That's almost as lame as the jokes Dad tells," Madison said.

Mom held up the dress. "We'll take it!" she told the store clerk, a young girl with blue streaks in her hair who reminded Madison of Mariah.

What with the fun visit to Mom's office, the taxi rides, and the purple dress, the trip into New York was classifiable as nothing short of a success. Despite the false Will-sighting, Madison was happier than happy about the way the day turned out. Later that night, after a long, rush-hour train ride home, she wrote about all of their exploits in her files. Luckily for Madison, Gramma Helen was sleeping in the den on this trip, not in Madison's bedroom, where she normally camped out on her visits. That meant Madison could stretch across her bed and go online.

After being away in the city for an entire day, Madison half-expected to find a huge windfall of e-communication waiting for her. How weird not to have spoken with any of her BFFs or other classmates that day! Surprisingly, however, no one had sent any mail, not even Bigwheels or Aimee, not even Ivy, writing to touch base about tomorrow's science presentation. There wasn't even any spam. And there were no text messages on her cell phone, either.

Trying hard not to feel super discouraged, Madison sent out a text message of her own. Just as she was composing it, her phone beeped.

A message! At last!

Madison hit SAVE for the message she'd just written and moved to her text-message in-box, where she entered the READ MESSAGES prompt.

Is yr e-mail down? missed u @ school SO how's yr science thing? Chet & I r working 2nite text me asap H

Madison grinned at the letter *H*.

Hart was thinking of her? He *missed* her?

Somehow, that short little message gave Madison a very big boost. She typed a quick hello back so Hart

180

knew she was thinking about him and then sat down on her bed with a bunch of Mom's old magazines, a pair of scissors, and some glue. It was time she began work on her Blue Sky collage.

There were only a few days of school left, but Madison Francesca Finn was newly determined to make the most of them.

Chapter 15

Wednesday was P-Day.

Somehow the night before, even after the long day in the city, Madison had found the time to rip out some pictures of blue, cloudless skies from mom's old magazines and make a collage from the scraps, pasting words like *spectrum* and *refraction* and *scattered light* in different areas. In one corner was a rainbow; in another was a bright sun with rays. Mr. Danehy would be impressed. At least, Madison hoped so.

Overnight, she'd developed a game plan, which wasn't exactly revenge, but close. Madison had figured that she would try to present as much information as possible and then leave Ivy to answer the questions from Mr. Danehy. From experience,

Madison knew that that was how he liked to work things. He liked any chance to quiz students on what they'd learned. Ivy would fall flat on her face during that part, for sure! She would be the one looking dumb, not Madison.

When science class came, Madison put her plan into action. Poster in hand, she explained how light was scattered by oxygen when it hit the atmosphere, and how blue light was absorbed the most readily.

"It's not that the sky is painted or colored blue, exactly," Madison explained, pointing to parts of her diagram. "It's just that that's how our eyes see it. We see the blue light more than other colors."

"Very good, Ms. Finn," Mr. Danehy said.

Ivy kept trying to get a word in edgewise, but Madison talked right over her. When it came time to do one of the simple experiments, Madison stepped right in and worked with all of the items herself. She explained the theory of thin-film interference.

"This shows how a coating of nail polish in water takes white light that shines on it and turns it into different colors, like a rainbow. It's a lot like the white light that is absorbed in the sky. Depending on how the light is absorbed in the air, we see different shades of blue or whatever color. Depending on how thick or thin the nail polish is, we see different shades of color, too. . . ."

"Yeah, that's right," Ivy chimed in, beginning to look worried.

"Wow," Mr. Danehy said. "That was a good experiment for this scientific proof. I am impressed with the both of you—How hard you've worked!"

The both of us?

Ivy's momentary look of worry turned back into one of gloating. She was again getting all the credit for work she had not done.

To make matters worse, Mr. Danehy skipped over the Q & A portion. He said that all of his questions had already been answered. Madison was half tempted to expose Ivy right there, once and for all, but for some reason, she held back. When Mr. Danehy asked for the pair's detailed journal of observations and notes, Madison passed him the purple notebook with a polite smile and said, "Here's our journal. Can I get that back after you've reviewed it?"

Mr. Danehy nodded. "Thank you, Ms. Finn," he said, by his gestures encouraging the other students in class to applaud the presentation. Then Ivy had the steely nerve to take a bow in the middle of everything.

Out of the corner of her eye, Madison saw Hart looking her way, which was a very good thing. That alone kept her from bursting into tears on the spot. After all, Hart knew the truth.

At least someone in the room did.

After the day's classes, Madison headed to the second and final rehearsal with everyone from the musical revue. She had missed the rehearsal the day before, because she'd gone to New York City. As she walked into the auditorium, she felt weird and goose-pimply all over, like a stranger to the place, not one bit the way she had felt when she had been stage manager of the seventh-grade play. For that, she had a very important role, even if it was behind the scenes. This time, she was just a minor player in a huge production.

She probably wouldn't have felt quite so weird if the one and only revue performance hadn't been scheduled for that very night. But it was. And the performers and backstage helpers and others were buzzing like a beehive.

The longer she stood there, the more Madison's nerves felt as if they were about to *snap*. Where was she supposed to stand? She liked to be in charge, or at least to be in the know, but right now she had no idea where anything belonged. Who was singing or dancing? Where were all the decorative props? Did it even matter that she was there?

Madison looked to Hart for guidance, but he was off in the wings with some other boys, moving sets and signs.

Fiona had said she wasn't coming to rehearsal until late, so Aimee, Lindsay, and Madhur tried their best to calm Madison down and clue her in on what had happened at the rehearsal the day before, but that only frustrated Madison more. It seemed as if she had set herself up these last weeks of school to do all these fun things, and now she was lagging behind everyone else at the revue. And it wasn't just the revue. She was behind in Science, too, now that Ivy had turned into the über-genius, despite doing absolutely *no* work.

Gack.

There was so little time left before Moving Up Day—before seventh grade came to its screeching halt. Could she ever catch up? Madison looked around at the other kids. Did they really know what was going on, or were they just faking it—the way Ivy usually did?

"Hey, Finnster," Hart said, appearing by her side.

It was the right guy at the right time. Without even thinking, Madison wrapped her arm around Hart's waist. She'd been flip-flopping all week long, but now she just wanted to hold on tight.

"Hey," Madison said.

"So, you got my messages?" Hart asked. "I was kinda worried. And when I saw you in science class today, you seemed a million miles away."

"It's just Ivy. She's the worst partner *ever*."

"She's a bonehead. Everyone knows it."

"Everyone?"

Hart nodded. "No doubt."

"I'm sorry if I seemed preoccupied lately," Madison said. "I didn't mean to be."

"Okay, I forgive you," Hart said with a smile. His

teeth looked really white and clean for some reason, like those of a guy on the cover of a magazine. His glasses had slipped down a little on his nose. Madison took her fingertip and pushed them up gently.

"You're back on props?" Madison asked.

Hart nodded. "Yeah."

"So maybe you can fill me in. Because I am totally *clueless*," Madison said with a laugh and an exaggerated toss of her head.

"Here's the master list. Mr. Montefiore passed it out yesterday," Hart said. "I got you an extra copy."

"You did?" Madison asked, surprised.

"I wanted to give it to you earlier, but then I didn't see you at lunch."

"Thanks," Madison said, taking the sheet.

Mrs. Montefiore hit a few sharp notes on the piano keys, and the final run-through officially began.

"Remember, boys and girls," Mrs. Montefiore said, "we're not going to do entire numbers. We just want you to take places, run through any major stage motions, and then we'll move right along to scene and number transitions. Got it?"

"Got it!" about three dozen kids yelled back. Then everyone participating from the seventh, eighth, and ninth grades ran to take their places, some backstage, some onstage, and some in the orchestra pit, or at least the section of floor next to the stage that served as a temporary pit. Madison followed the crowd like she was one of the sheep.

On a master list of performance numbers, Madison saw the names of songs, skits, and dances (many of which featured Aimee or Aimee's choreography). Madison scanned the list. How could they ever perform thirty numbers in only two hours?

Mrs. Montefiore played the piano a little louder.

"Now, we're opening the revue with 'There's No Business like Show Business,' right? So . . . why am I staring at an empty stage? Get up there, performers!" she shouted. "We only have a little time before the real thing! Let's go!"

A cluster of kids in shoes with taps clicked and clacked their way onto the stage. Most of them wore top hats, except for two kids at the end of a line.

"Hats!" Mrs. Montefiore shouted. She looked around for a prop person. Mariah was standing nearby. "Ah! Mariah! Where are those hats?"

Madison saw the look of momentary panic on Mariah's face. But instead of freaking out, she calmly nodded, as if to say, "Got it!" and raced offstage. A moment later, she was back again with the two missing black hats, each one decorated at the brim with silver sparkles.

Aimee and a couple of the other choreographers joined the line midway through the song. They were dressed in silver lamé shirts and black tights, with sneakers that had been spray-painted silver. Aimee strutted around the stage. Madison hadn't seen her dance, *really* dance, in a long time. Aimee had gotten so good this year. Her blond hair was piled loosely on her head and secured with silver barrettes, and she had on gobs of makeup, too, which made her look like some kind of real Broadway star.

After the opening number, a breathless crew of kids shuffled off the stage to loud applause. Mrs. Montefiore cheered the loudest of all, which put everyone in a better mood.

The next few songs required Madison's help—and she was eager to get to work and be a part of the action. Following the instructions on the list that Hart had given to her, Madison toted props to their designated places on the stage: three red telephones; a graffiti-covered guitar; fake flowers in fake pots; and a pile of papers. Hart and some other kids helped out with one of the bigger items, a bunch of oversize cutouts of skyscrapers needed for the United States tribute portion of the revue. In the half-darkness, the props team moved a fake field of oats and grass offstage and shuttled the city backdrop onto the stage, making the transition from the show tune "Oklahoma" to "New York, New York!" complete.

"Props aren't so bad," Hart whispered as he and Madison lowered their painted plywood Chrysler Building onto the stage. "I could get used to this."

"Thanks for switching back," Madison whispered.

Hart grinned, or at least Madison thought he had. She couldn't really tell; it was that dark out there. There was no doubt, however, about what

Hart did next. As they hurried offstage, he put his hand on the small of her back and pushed her ever so gently. Of course, he could have been saying, "Hurry up and move it!" But Madison preferred to think that Hart's touch was saying, "I like you, with a capital *L*, Madison Finn."

Either way, they were backstage again in a matter of seconds, and "New York, New York!" started up.

This was Ivy's big number, so Madison hung around to watch. According to Madhur, Fiona, and Aimee, when the rehearsals had first started, Ivy thought she was going onstage dressed as some kind of urban supermodel, with her red hair teased up and out, and wearing a long dress and heels. Instead, she ended up as the Statue of Liberty, and had to sing her song dressed from head to toe in green, holding a torch in one hand and an encyclopedia in the other.

Ivy was trying to make the most of it; Madison could tell. And Madison was rooting for her, too, for some reason. She hated to see anyone, even the enemy, get embarrassed by a performance. After all, Madison understood jitters and stage fright better than anyone.

But all her good wishes did no good. Ivy strutted her stuff out onto the center of the stage, but on the way there she got tripped up in her green cloak. One moment she was striding forward, head thrown back like a princess's. The next moment, she fell, fast and hard.

Ivy's fall gave new meaning to the word *splat*, but somehow she scrambled back up again and smoothed out her clothes.

"Did someone leave something on the stage?" Ivy called out.

"Props!" Mr. Montefiore cried from the auditorium.

Madison was the closest prop person to the site of the accident. She raced onstage and immediately found herself a little disoriented. She glanced out into the audience. The lights temporarily blinded her. But then some kid turned up the houselights, and everyone could see everything.

"Now, this is a big number," Mr. Montefiore said, gesticulating in exasperation. "So far, this rehearsal is about fifty percent there, and we need *better*. We can't have props lying around. Could everyone who's backstage please come out for a moment? We need a cast powwow."

Mr. Montefiore lectured for about ten minutes, during which Madison had to bite her tongue to keep from laughing. All around, it seemed as though her friends were trying to make her laugh, from Hart (making goofy faces) to Madhur (nonstop eye-rolling). There was something funny and nerve-racking about it all at the same time.

Aimee rushed over. "What did you think?"

"You were fabulous," Madison quickly said, "but someone else's dance movements could use a little help. . . ."

"You mean Miss Green?" Aimee joked. "Yeah, she's not exactly a ballerina. She should ·stick to being mean and stealing boys."

"Excuse me?"

Madison and Aimee whipped around and saw Ivy, still clad in her Statue of Liberty outfit, standing there.

"I heard what you just said," Ivy snarled.

"So?" Aimee shot back.

"So, I think you're rude and cruel and unusual," Ivy said.

"Unusual?" Aimee repeated. "Doink."

Madison started to giggle. "*We're* rude? *We're* cruel?"

Ivy looked indignant. "You're not supposed to laugh at people when they're down."

Madison didn't know what to say. Was Ivy serious? Ivy was the queen of knocking people when they were down. Was she *that* out of touch with reality? Or was she just playing Madison for a fool . . . again? Ivy looked ready to cry, but Ivy Daly *never* cried.

Just then, one of the ninth-grade boys in charge of the backstage area rushed over.

"Um . . ." he stammered. "We can hear everything you say out on the stage, you know? The side mics are still turned on."

bur...

Ivy, on... ...mediately felt her cheeks start to her face. Her e, ...dramatic sniff as the..., suddenly got a sly look on the side mics. Then she ... d to tear up. She gave a direction. ... ...er went to turn off ... in the opposite

"Faker," Aimee said after Ivy ran o...

Madison remained silent. She was thinki... Was Ivy just messing with them to get sympathy from the other kids? And teachers?

Just then, Fiona ran up to Madison.

"Maddie, I heard everything out front. We all did. What happened?" Fiona asked.

"I don't know," Madison said. "I guess Ivy had on a microphone, and she fell and . . . I feel kind of bad."

"You should *not* feel bad," Aimee said.

"What else did I miss?" Fiona asked. "I wish I'd been to rehearsal on time."

"Why *are* you late?" Aimee asked.

"My dad," Fiona grumbled.

"What about your dad?" Madison asked.

"Oh, he wanted me and Chet to stay home this afternoon so we could meet this guy he works with. I think it might be his new boss. Dad's been interviewing for that important job on the West Coast I told you guys about."

"In California, right?" Madison said.

Fiona nodded. "He's flown ~~w times.
This guy works in an offi~~ttan, though.
He needed to meet Da~~eally going to move?"
"So, you think y~~u'll move too, right?"
Aimee asked. "I~~ Fiona said. "He never really
"I guess. ~~g. Neither does Mom."
tells us an~~eemed super secretive all of a sudden.
Fio~~on wondered why.
Ma

"Fiona, I know I keep saying this, but you'd tell us if your family was really planning to move, wouldn't you?" Madison asked.

"Totally!" Fiona said. "You guys are my BFFs. You'd be the first to know."

"Hey, who's in the 'Corner of the Sky' song?" some kid yelled out backstage. "We're missing the green and yellow leotards."

Aimee let out a gasp and ran off. Fiona started to move away, too, but Madison grabbed her hand.

"You can't move back to California, Fiona," she said dejectedly. "Not when I just found out my dad is moving, too."

"Your dad is moving?" Fiona said. "Wow. Where?"

"A half hour away. Into a house. He says he and Stephanie will still be close to Far Hills and New York, but I don't want him to go anywhere. . . ."

"I don't know, Maddie," Fiona said with a shrug. "Dads can be so weird about moving and all that. Like mine, for instance. He hasn't told me everything that

"W

Madison as... Chet and I know something's up." your dad has ...eave your house in Far Hills?" chased away the gho...e that old Victorian, and ...ed it up, and we even

"Yeah," Fiona chuckled.

Madison and Fiona heard a pi..." badly out of tune onstage. Something crashed. It... ...ded like a thousand nails scattered upon the stage at ...ce.

"What *was* that?" Madison asked.

"Places! Places!" someone shouted.

A few kids elbowed their way past Madison and Fiona onto the stage. *"Do, a deer, a female deer . . . Re, a drop of golden sun . . . Mi, a name I call myself . . . Fa, a long, long way to run . . ."* Some of the kids were singing a chorus from *The Sound of Music.*

"Do, re, mi, fa, so, la, ti, Do-o-o-o-o-o-o!"

"No-o-o-o-o-o!" Mrs. Montefiore screamed out in the auditorium; she didn't sound happy. The last note of that chorus had been more than a little bit off key.

Mariah raced by, and Madison grabbed her arm.

"What's going on out there?" Madison asked.

Mariah grabbed her hair by its pink streaks and broke into maniacal laughter. "It's the end of the world as we know it!" she cried, half joking.

Madison felt a case of the nervous giggles coming on.

And the actual revue performance was only two hours away.

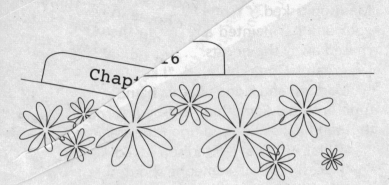

 Friends till the End

I guess the saying goes that a bad dress rehearsal means a great performance.

We were no exception. The revue rocked.

Every prop was put onstage at the right time. No one was too off key (except for this one 8th grader named Evan something who sounded like a sick garbage truck when he sang). The biggest surprise of all: Ivy didn't fall in her ugly green Statue of Liberty dress. She actually got a standing O. Go figure. Even *I* was clapping. Poison Ivy belted out these few high notes like she was some kind of Mariah Carey wannabe, g...

enemy.

...ly worked. Hey, gotta give a
...ven if she IS the mortal

Fiona... nailed her so...
never seems to ge... always, too. She
like this. Lindsay wa... know why, but she
song (w/Fiona, actually), ...up about things
small solo part and she sounde... erforming one
fine. She looked so good in stage... had a
like a model. Aimee danced and spun he... than
through all her musical numbers just lik... up,
she wanted, and she got a lot of claps at ... way
the end. I bet she really does become a pro
dancer someday. She sure likes all the
attention. Madhur wasn't a bad dancer,
although she kept laughing during some of
the songs when she couldn't *quite* keep up.
Even I, queen of the nonperformers, know
that you have to keep your composure when
you're onstage. One thing's for sure: those
four are my super pals. I felt so proud.
Wait. Does that make me sound like some
kind of weird mommy hen? Er . . . cluck!

No, no, here's what's REALLY weird: Mr.
and Mrs. Montefiore both cried (yes, I did
say cried) at the end of the entire revue.
It was some serious soap-opera stuff, I
swear. These ninth-grade kids (incl. Egg's
sis, Mariah), who've been doing this for 3
years, brought them these huge bouquets of
sunflowers at the very end. My mom and dad
(sitting in--NEWSFLASH--the same section!)
both told me there wasn't a dry eye in the

197

place. I'd be willing . t either.
however, that Mariah ...ing too much time
I have to admit tiways-cynical Aim and
Wow. Have I ...y did I never really get
these days wi revue thing? I would have
Maddie One? end the year as a blubbering
into the expect...ting emotional about everything
fool...veryone at the drop of a hat. But
an...stead, I feel weirdly stuck in this *muck*.

Rude Awakening: My birth certificate
says Madison Francesca Finn, but my real
name is MUD.

MUD (aka Moving Up Day) means I'm
graduating. I survived seventh grade! But
I feel sadder than sad. Why does the most
important day of my life mean I have to
say good-bye?

Madison hit SAVE and surfed to her e-mailbox. It
was still early on Thursday morning, so she had time
to mess around on the computer a little bit. This was
a good way to calm her nerves, which had been fully
frazzled since the previous day. She would take her
time that morning, carefully putting on her new purple dress, fixing her hair in a pretty twist, and slowly
gathering together everything else she needed to
bring to school, like Thank You and Good-bye cards
for all of her favorite teachers. Madison didn't have
to call Aimee and Fiona for at least a half hour or

more. Th⌐
three BFFs, plu⌐ ⌐en Mom would be driving the
for MUD. The par⌐. brother, Chet, over to school
Despite getting ⌐⌐igh, were invited for later.
Madison wasn't the only ⌐re anyone that day,
chronic case of nerves. Mom ⌐n her house with a
fully stretched rubber band. And ⌐⌐ wound up as a
was probably downstairs at that mo⌐ ⌐ison knew she
the house ready for guests *and* gettin⌐ ⌐nt, getting
snap. She'd been anxious about the party ⌐or a
while. Now that the actual day had arrived, Mom
was channeling her anxiety into Clorox, Ajax, and
Windex. She'd gone into cleanup overdrive. The air
inside the house reeked of bleach and pine. In that
situation, the best thing to do (other than volunteering to vacuum or dust) was to steer clear.

Gramma Helen knew how to steer *way* clear. She
turned all of her attention away from Mom and
toward Phin. Madison could hear her grandmother
and her pug just then in the kitchen, making cooing
noises at each other. Gramma was probably giving
Phinnie too many of the little bacon doggy treats he
loved so much—the ones that made his belly fat.
And Phin was probably dancing around on his hind
legs, begging for more.

The rest of Madison's family members had
arrived the previous evening, but Madison wouldn't
be seeing them until the official start time of the
party, which was around four o'clock. Uncle Rick and

Aunt Violet had spent the ~~~night with Dad
and Stephanie at their ~~~nt. Uncle Bob and
Aunt Angie were co~~eting ~~o Far Hills on a mid-
morning flight. For~~r moment, Stephanie
seemed to think~~r niece and nephew might
come from Tex~~or a special trip (and for the big
occasion), b~~hey had their own moving-up and
graduation~~eremonies to attend back home.

Mad~~on clicked on her e-mailbox to see if she'd
gotten any mail since the last time she had checked.
There were at least ten spam e-mails in there. But
there was one e-mail, from Madison's keypal.

```
From: Bigwheels
To: MadFinn
Subject: Hey, hey we're moving UP
Date: Wed 21 Jun 10:10 PM
```
One more day and we are soooo outta
here. Same goes 4 u2, right? I
think u said u guys had a big
ceremony and party. We just get
certificates @ the end of school,
last period. Really no big whoop,
but having an official piece of
paper makes it seem cool somehow.

Did u ever get the perfect dress? I
actually decided 2 wear pants and
this cute top, very bohemian with
beaded earrings and necklace my mom

got me a[t] the cool discount store. They
have the co~~ol~~ discount store. won't be the p~~riciest~~ outfits. I know I
class, but I th~~inn~~iest girl in my
ten. Is that totall~~y~~ I'm in the top
I'm just feeling good ~~v~~ain of me?
the real reason why: REG~~gie~~. Forget
that other Matt guy. Reggie is back
on the front burner. He brought me
REAL flowers when he picked me up
4 the seventh-grade dance. They
haven't even wilted yet and it's 2
days later. It was sooo romantic
and totally off the charts.

I hope ur feeling good 2. U
SHOULD!!! We are 8th graders now
& how totally cool is that??? I'm
in a TOTAL school daze. We're that
much closer 2 high school. I know
we're not supposed 2 rush it, but
I can't help but feel a teeny bit
more mature now. Doncha think?

Yours till the graduation caps,

Vicki aka Bigwheels

p.s.: We finally named our pony
Tony. The name was my little
brother's idea. A girl pony named

Tony?!! Oh well. I love horses
beautiful animals make me think of
because they a'the sunset. Bye!!!
riding off in

Madison hit SAVE and then REPLY. Bigwheels had
the best timing. What could Madison write back that
would be just as special to read and enjoy before
graduation?

From: MadFinn
To: Bigwheels
Subject: Re: Hey, hey we're moving UP
Date: Thurs 22 Jun 7:28 AM

I'm sitting here with my laptop,
about 2 get in2 this VERY COOL AND
AMAZING purple dress that I bought
esp. 4 2day. And BTW: I have NO
probs with yr bragging. Y shouldn't
u brag? Ur a fox, right? (Cue the
growl sound, pls.) LOL

I'm glad yr end-of-school dance went
well. U and Reggie sound A+ 4 each
other. My boy sitch is same as
ever, maybe a smidge better than
the same. I think that turtle camp
guy will stay a friend but Hart
will stay in my heart. That sounds
like one of yr poems, right? I've

des~
thru a~ at Hart and I are
7th grade ~ch other. We've been
fm high schoo~ther grades and now
At least I'm thin~ollege together.
~ll prob. graduate
~that. Y not?

N e way, I'll E you aga~
the whole big MUD--if I do~after
too messy. LOL (for like the ~th get
time in this e-mail). I'm a little
silly. Nerves about 2day. BLAAHHHH!

E ya 18r?

Yours till the school daze (b/c I'm
in one 2),

Maddie

p.s.: I don't think Tony the Pony
is THAT bad a name. We call one of
Poison Ivy's drones Phony Joanie;
and it's a good rhyme, right? So
how many animals r in yr family
now? Phinnie would do a dog flip
out if we got another critter. He
likes being an only dog as much
as I like being an only child
(even tho I say I don't like it
sometimes).

After hitting SEND and ... ⌐ging off, Madison surfed around bi⌐ ...om a little bit. Then, she noticed an u⌐ ...note in her drafts folder. What was this⌐at she checked, she found the barely there e-⌐at she'd started for Will the week before. ...eleted this like a hundred times,"

"I thoug⌐ ...ned to herself. But maybe this was a Madison c⌐ad to deal with it—and with Will. sign. S⌐

Madison opened the old e-mail and rewrote the date.

```
From: MadFinn
To: WillPOWR
Subject: Re: Remember me?
Date: Thurs 22 Jun 7:32 AM
```
Sorry I didn't write
backkkkkkkkkkkkkk

Madison's finger stuck on the *K* key. She paused and stared at the screen. What exactly should she say to this boy? She kept typing, trusting that the right words would just come.

```
Sorry I didn't write back sooner.
I was caught in a major storm in
the middle of the Bermuda Triangle
```

Yeah, that was believable. Bermuda Triangle. Good one. She started again.

Sorry I didn't write back sooner.
I didn't know what to say when I
got yr e-mail. It made me happy.
Actually, I was in the city the
other day w/my mom and gramma and
I kept looking around, wondering
if I would c u on the street. LOL.
N e way, I am so glad ur out there
and YES I would like to stay in
touch. Right now I'm getting ready
for our moving-up ceremony 2 8th
grade. Can we E each other over
the summer?

WBS.

Madison read it over. And then she read it once more. It was simple enough. It made sense. It wasn't too hot or cold; it was *juuuuust* right, just like Baby Bear's porridge in *Goldilocks and the Three Bears.* So, after all the waiting and wondering, Madison had finally made up her mind. Unlike some of the songs in the musical revue, this message was pitch-perfect.

Madison stared as the screen put up the message showing that her message had been successfully sent. It was as easy—and as fast—as that. Now all she had to do was wait for Will's next move (and message). That would probably mean another round of wondering and waiting, but that was okay. She had other important things on her mind—like Hart.

"Maddie!"

Mom called up from downstairs. Madison could hear the tension in her voice.

"Maddie, are you up there? I need your help!"

Madison had always said her middle name was Help. The same had been true at the beginning, middle, and, now, the end of seventh grade. For all the things that changed a lot, there were still some things that remained status quo.

"What is it, Mom?" Madison yelled back. Her voice echoed in the hall.

"I said I need you! Come down, now!"

Madison snapped the top of her laptop closed and shuffled out to the steps in her slippers. "What is it?" she called from the top of the stairs.

Mom stood below, yellow rubber gloves on her hands, a bucket of soapy water at her feet, and holding a red-striped rag.

"Maddie, you are trying my patience, do you know that?"

Madison bit her lip. "Sorry," she mumbled. "What is it?"

"I just need you to help me set out some things on the dining-room table," Mom said in a softer voice. "I'm sorry, too, I don't mean to yell. I just—"

Madison was at the bottom of the steps by then. She reached out for Mom's arm. "I know,

206

Mom, you're stressed. It's the party. It's the family. I know."

Mom looked as if she were about to cry, but she didn't. She sat down in an upholstered chair, peeled off her gloves, and just sighed. "This is your special day," she said, wiping her brow.

"Let's just put the stuff out and get through it," Madison said. "It's really no biggie, Mom."

They went into the dining room and set out the plates, decorations, silverware, and serving dishes. It only took a few, easy minutes. Gramma and Phin helped, too, by continuing to steer clear. They stayed in the kitchen the whole time.

"You'd better go get ready now," Mom said. "Today we need to be on time."

Madison nodded, leaned close to give Mom a kiss, and headed back upstairs. This time, Phin barked and followed behind her, leaving Gramma and Mom to work out the details of the next cleaning task.

The purple MUD dress still fit perfectly. Madison slipped right into it without any problem, although she quickly sniffed her armpits, just to make sure she wasn't stinky from all the nervousness. Then she slid on a pair of black flats and a chunky armful of bracelets, a secret tribute to the style of her favorite teacher, Mrs. Wing.

"You look fantabulous," Gramma Helen said from the bedroom doorway. Madison nearly jumped out of her skin; she hadn't know anyone was watching.

"Is 'fantabulous' a real word?" Madison asked. It didn't sound like a Gramma Helen kind of word at all.

Gramma just shrugged and chuckled. "Oh, go ask a dictionary. I'm just your grandmother."

They both laughed. Sometimes Gramma was so serious, but other times she liked to be goofy. Those times always cracked Madison up.

Channeling her inner hairdresser, Gramma helped Madison to pull her brown hair into a thick, black barrette. Then Madison put on her favorite moonstone earrings, the lucky ones Dad had given to her a year before. They matched the dress and hairdo perfectly. Her outfit was complete.

Madison looked at her reflection in the mirror. The morning sunlight was coming into her room at just the right angle, and it reflected back off the glass, making a kind of white halo around Madison's head, except at the beveled edges of the mirror, where the bent light reflected a full spectrum of color. It was as if Madison were the science project right now, caught in refracted light, at the epicenter of a rainbow.

"You do look beautiful this morning," Gramma said, complimenting her again. "I'm so glad I could be here to share this special day with you."

"Thanks," Madison turned around and grinned.

"I better go call Aim and Fiona now. I think I'm finally ready to jump in the MUD."

Gramma Helen flashed her dentures and let out a belly laugh. "Oh, Madison! You truly are my one and only," she said.

Chapter 17

As Mom pulled into the school building parking lot with Madison, Aimee, Fiona, and Chet clustered in the back of the Finn van, the air felt electric.

The day they'd all been waiting for had arrived.

The FHJH school building stood larger than life with its wide double doors at the front entrance. Today, it wasn't overrun with screaming kids and teachers, buses pulling in and out, or car doors slamming open and shut. There was no front-of-building security guard standing watch over the crowds. Kids wandered in as if they were heading into a movie theater or something, talking in much chattier tones than usual and greeting each other with high fives and handshakes. It was like a foreign place in some ways, and the mood was definitely set for celebrating. Madison was happy to be there, decked out in her purple dress and lucky moonstones.

"Yo!" Egg cried from across the hallway when the girls and Chet walked inside the school.

Fiona rushed over. Madison and Aimee followed. Unlike the relatively calm mood outside, the atmosphere inside was busy. There was a large table set up in the lobby. On it sat a yellow paper program for the moving-up ceremonies. The FHJH logo, a racehorse, was emblazoned across the front, along with the school motto: TOGETHER WE BUILD SUCCESS.

"I can't believe it's really here," Madison told her friends. "The end."

"The *beginning*," Fiona corrected her.

Aimee seemed distracted. "Have you guys seen Ben anywhere?"

Aimee's crush had been chosen to speak on behalf of the class, and she seemed nervous.

"Bathroom," Madhur said.

Everyone laughed.

"Don't forget, Ivy's giving a speech, too," Aimee reminded Madison.

"What?" Madison cried. "Since when?"

"Since always," Chet spoke up. "She's the class president after all."

"Yeah, Maddie," Egg added. "Where have you been?"

Madison punched Egg in the arm.

"Hey," Egg cried. "Just because you hate her

211

doesn't mean you have to take it out on me!"

Fiona, Aimee, and the others chuckled.

"I really do hate her," Madison declared bitterly. She usually didn't say things that sounded quite so harsh, but Ivy had made her madder than mad. She'd wreaked havoc on Madison's final weeks of school. Now Madison had to listen to Ivy give some self-important class president speech? There was nothing worse.

Bit by bit, the school got more crowded. Kids headed to their homerooms to congregate, but Madison and her friends decided to stay together in the hall, searching for signs of intelligent life— namely, Madhur and Lindsay. Madison spotted Madhur first, wearing a dress made from yellow and red Indian scarves. She looked like some kind of Punjabi princess. Lindsay looked good, too, although she had on a purple dress just like Madison's.

"Did you guys coordinate your outfits, or what?" Madhur asked.

Madison and Lindsay both laughed. "Yeah," they joked at the same time, locking arms at the elbow. "We're practically like twins, remember?"

Lindsay smiled. "You're all sort of like sisters to me," she said.

"So-o-o sappy!" Aimee cried, but she smiled at the same time.

"Like you don't say sappy stuff," Madhur said, nudging her.

Madison reached into her orange bag and pulled out one of the special items she'd brought just for that day: a digital camera. Dad had lent her his.

"Smile!" Madison said, raising the camera and aiming it at her pals. True to form, the four of them huddled together with arms entwined.

"Why don't you let me take your picture with them?" someone from behind Madison said. She whirled around to see Hart standing there.

"Hey, you," Madison said, grabbing him by the arm. She handed him the camera. "Thanks."

"You look um . . . *pretty* today," Hart whispered in Madison's ear as he took the camera. Madison glanced around to see if anyone else had heard the compliment, but everyone was having their own conversations, and no one was paying Madison and Hart any mind.

"Well, thanks again," Madison whispered back.

Just then, the loudspeaker boomed. Principal Bernard was announcing the countdown to the big ceremony.

"Attention, Far Hills students and families. Welcome to our school today for a tremendous celebration of another successful year. We'll be starting the ceremonies in approximately fifteen minutes. Faculty, please lead students into the main auditorium. Guests should also turn in your tickets and take your seats. Please turn off your cell phones."

Everything about the walk back down the hall

and into the auditorium made Madison's head spin. Hart stayed closer than close to her side the whole time, which made her feel secure for some reason. Seeing Hart today confirmed that she'd made the right choice between him and Will.

Aimee let out a low holler and waved madly across the room. She saw her mom, her dad, and two of her four brothers coming inside, and she wanted them to know where she was sitting. Lindsay, Madhur, and Fiona saw their families and flagged them down.

Madison didn't have any such luck. She knew Mom and Gramma Helen and Dad and Stephanie *had* to be out there somewhere, but she didn't hear Mom's familiar "Honey bear?" or Dad's bellowed "My Maddie!" It would have been so like Dad to do something embarrassing (like scream Madison's name and get everyone in the room to stop and stare). He was good for lousy jokes and behavior like that sometimes. Still, he wasn't there yet; that much was clear.

Down in the orchestra pit, the Far Hills String Ensemble joined in with members of the school band to play the Allegro from Handel's *Concerti Grossi*. Some notes sounded a little sharp, like nails on a chalkboard, but overall, the music was good. Madison wondered why she'd slacked off so much that year on her flute-playing. She could have been a band member, too. Maybe next year?

214

Quicker than Madison ever expected, Principal Bernard started the moving-up ceremony by having everyone in the crowd sing the school song. Of course, he was louder than most folks, since he sang into a microphone, and unfortunately, his pitch was way off. Madison and a bunch of other kids sank down into the auditorium seats and tried to tune out rather than sing along. They'd only sung it maybe twice during the entire year. So some of the words were missing. She'd have to learn the entire thing the following year, in eighth grade.

After the last chorus, Assistant Principal Goode scurried up to the microphone with a long sheet of paper in her hand.

"Good morning," she announced in a chipper tone. "We have some special speakers to start our program. After that, we will move to the awards and recognition part of the ceremony. Our teachers will present deserving students with certificates and awards for their academic and extracurricular endeavors."

Madison shot a look at Fiona. They'd only recently been gabbing about how much Fiona deserved the team award for soccer. Madison hoped that her friend would get it—and everything else she deserved.

The first special speaker up to the podium was none other than Ben Buckley. Aimee leaned back in a swoon, as usual, upon seeing him come onstage. Lindsay and Madhur made a jokey comment about Ben's starched shirt, baggy pants, and haircut (or lack thereof). But Aimee didn't seem to mind his appearance. She hung on Ben's every word.

"Good morning." Ben started his speech in a low, rumbly voice. "When the teachers asked me to . . . er . . . talk to everyone today, I didn't know how to start. I'm not even sure if you all know me. . . ."

A brief titter passed through the audience. Madison turned around and saw that it was a group of eighth graders—the cool clique, no doubt—making the ruckus. But they didn't do it for long.

Ben cleared his throat but continued, undeterred.

"Anyway, my favorite teacher, Mr. Gibbons, says that everywhere in life we face challenges, even in seventh grade. And they are important, no matter what anyone says. They are important because they matter to us. Principal Bernard says on the loudspeaker every Friday that we have to find the steady path and stay focused in school. We have to figure things out. I was thinking about this poem by Robert Frost. He says, *'I took the road less traveled by, and that has made all the difference. . . .'*"

Ben paused, and some kid called out, "What road was that? Ridge or Poplar?"

The room erupted in a roar of laughter. Even a few parents chuckled, but order was restored quickly.

"Why did someone make fun of him in the middle of his speech?" Aimee whispered, indignant. "It's

216

because Ben sounds a little intense, right? I mean, for a seventh grader."

"Yeah! It's not like he's the president giving a State of the Union speech or something," Madhur said.

"Oh," Aimee sighed. "Poor Ben."

"No!" Madison said, defending him. "Ben sounds really, really smart. Don't let those pranksters mess with your head. He sounds good. Look. Principal Bernard is all ears."

Aimee smiled. Madison hoped that despite Ben's total geekiness, Aimee knew that no one thought she was crazy for liking him. Aimee's "like" for Ben was even *more* admirable than anything she might have felt for some slick soccer dude.

Moments later, Ben finished his speech, but not before tossing in a few more important lines—that quoted everyone from Green Day to former president Clinton. At the end, the auditorium burst into loud applause. Thankfully, the few bad apples who had mocked Ben early in the speech didn't make a fuss now.

Principal Bernard gave another of his short little speeches, and then a dazzling Mrs. Wing approached the podium. She wore one of her favorite scarves that had little sequins and mirrors sewn into it, so when she stepped under the spotlight, she literally shone. First, Mrs. Wing showed a short, candid slide show of kids from all over the school, and then she reminded everyone in the room about their memory pages. Madison was bummed when the teacher didn't mention her "team," but time was tight, so she didn't. And no sooner had Mrs. Wing rushed away than the next speaker took the stage.

Ivy Daly.

When Madison saw Poison Ivy stride up the stage steps, hips swinging from side to side, in one of her usual color-coordinated, label-conscious outfits, she wanted to yelp, "No-o-o-o-o-o-o-o!" How could anyone be fooled into thinking that this girl deserved the rank of Class Prez / Super Hot Chick / Coolest Clique Leader in the Seventh Grade? It was like one of Dad's awful jokes come to life. Ivy's way-too-short skirt belonged anywhere but in school, and yet, somehow she worked it; Madison was pretty sure she'd seen the skirt on the pages of a recent issue of *Star Beat.* Ivy was always brave enough to wear a skirt just *that much* teenier than everyone else's. And how did she get away with wearing tops that were *that much* tighter than anybody else's and shoes that were *that much* higher, too?

As Assistant Principal Goode introduced the seventh-grade class president, more titters passed through the crowd. But Madison didn't have to look very far to find the source of those.

"Aim!" Madison said in hushed tones. "Be quiet, or you'll get us all in trouble."

Aimee made a face. "*No* one heard me except you," she chided.

"I bet *Ben* heard," Madison shot back.

Aimee ignored Madison's comment and leaned way back in her auditorium seat.

By now, Ivy stood at the center of the stage. She was wearing makeup—a *lot* of makeup, as Madison could tell. Why was Ivy always trying to look and act so much older than she really was? Did she feel a need to keep pace with her older sister, Janet?

"Hey, there, everyone," Ivy said as she started her own speech. "Friends, parents, grandparents . . . First of all, I have to *totally* thank everyone for making me class president and making this year at Far Hills the best ever."

"She is *so* fake," Fiona grumbled. Once upon a time, way back at the start of school, Fiona had been friends with Ivy, for about five minutes. But that had been a shorter than short relationship.

"Fake isn't the word for it," Madhur grumbled back. "She's a poser. I mean, would someone please tell me exactly what she does as president? Did I miss something?"

Lindsay laughed out loud at that comment, which then caused a dozen people in the rows ahead of her—and some of the teachers a little farther down—to turn their heads in curiosity.

Sorry, Lindsay mouthed to anyone who glared or cared.

Madison tried really hard to pay attention, but she quickly gave up. What was the point? All year long, Madison and Ivy had been batting mean words and mean deeds back and forth. Nothing Ivy said would ever change that, especially not some kissy-face "I'm-just-so-sweet-how-can-you-*stand*-it?" speech prepared for the benefit of teachers and parents.

"Okay," Ivy said, "so I had no clue whatsoever about what to say. I'm so flattered to speak on behalf of all of you, as your class president and honorary member of the drama club. . . ."

Madison let out a grunt. "Please tell me she didn't just say that. She's so pathetic. . . ."

"Anyway, my parents gave me this twenty-dollar bill," Ivy continued.

"Twenty bucks?" Madison turned to Aimee. "And this information is supposed to matter to us . . . *how*?"

Aimee just rolled her eyes. "Don't look at me. I just go to school here."

Ivy continued. "Then they crumpled up the money. Can you *imagine*? And I said, 'Dad, why did you do that?' and he said, 'Ivy, you need to know something big: no matter what happens to you, your value and worth never changes. I can try to mark up and wrinkle this twenty dollars, but it will always be a twenty-dollar bill.'"

Madison realized that what Ivy said actually made sense. Aimee must have thought so, too, because she nudged Madison in the ribs.

"That's not such a terrible story, is it?" Aimee whispered.

Madison shook her head. "Not at all. Go figure. And I wanted to hate Ivy and her speech so much today. Oh, well . . ."

The loud applause at the end of Ivy's speech signaled an overall consensus in the room. As Gramma Helen would have said, Ivy had delivered the goods.

Then Principal Bernard went back up to the microphone and introduced the eighth-grade class speakers. Madison had no idea who these students were. The eighth-grade valedictorian was some girl named Chauncy who wore a fedora and talked about how important it was to be different. As far as Madison was concerned, Chauncy was trying way *too* hard to be different—from her name to her hat. Meanwhile, the eighth-grade class president was a boy named Omar, who talked about "believing the dream." Aimee summed up the speeches best when she said she felt like a waffle, drowning in syrup.

Madison wondered again if she and her friends were all being too judgmental. After all, what would people say if *Madison* had gotten on the stage to speak? Or Madhur? Or Fiona?

After a round of applause for the speakers, Principal Bernard motioned to Mrs. Goode to assist him in the awards portion of the ceremony. They were running twenty minutes behind schedule.

"Thank you once again to all of our brave, wise, and wonderful seventh and eighth graders," Principal Bernard said. "And now, without further ado, let's begin the really fun part of today's Moving Up Day bonanza. . . ."

Some kid from the drama club wheeled out a cart loaded with little miniature trophies, colored silk ribbons, and a big pile of certificates on embossed paper.

"First and foremost, we want to award the student with the best academic record. Of course, you have met both of our honorees today: Mr. Ben Buckley and Ms. Chauncy Rivers."

Principal Bernard was good under the gun. He wasted no time getting down to business and reading off the important names. Of course, that didn't prohibit him from telling a bad joke or two in between.

"Why is school like a shower?" he cracked. "One wrong turn and you're in hot water!"

The audience laughed politely. Madison heard one laugh that was louder than all the others and her belly flip-flopped.

Dad was out there.

Only Jeff Finn would laugh *that* hard at such a lame joke.

Aimee knew it, too. "So I guess your dad is here," she said, grinning.

Madison craned her neck to see if she could tell where Dad was sitting, but she didn't see him.

Principal Bernard was already passing out the next awards. He gave out individual achievement ribbons, and then moved on to sports awards, passing out trophies for best team players in each of the school sports. Egg was perched on the edge of his seat when it came time for the hockey trophy, but that went to some eighth grader who played goalie. When the time came to announce the girls' soccer awards, Madison crossed her fingers *and* toes.

"And the award for best soccer player goes to two people this year . . . Daisy Espinoza and Fiona Waters!"

Madison practically leaped out of her seat. She was very happy for Fiona, and wistful at the same time. What if this was the last assembly with her? She hoped Fiona wouldn't be moving all the way back to California. It would be sadder than sad.

The final part of the awards was reserved for a special new category, which Principal Bernard introduced as the Far Hills Project. It was really just a bunch of gobbledygook, as far as Madison was concerned, something about best academic efforts on school projects. The awards had been chosen and were to be distributed by selected faculty members.

It didn't seem fair to give him *all* the kudos on MUD, but Ben Buckley won yet another award for his work in Mr. Gibbons's English class. When Mrs. Wing stepped up to hand out a computer science nod, Egg turned to Madison with his thumb in the air and mouthed the words *You totally have this one!*

Of course, Madison wasn't surprised, or upset, a moment later when it was not her name that Mrs. Wing read at all. Instead, an eighth grader got the nod for her work on the school Web site's polling section.

Mr. Danehy stood up to hand out a science award. He had on a bow tie, and for some reason that made Madison giggle. Seeing him up there—goofy bow tie or not—made her feel a deep sense of relief, as though he were a symbol of everything that was over, really over, between Madison and seventh grade. He was definitely a symbol of what was over between Madison and Ivy; that was for sure.

"My science groups in seven and eight did outstanding work this year," Mr. Danehy said, taking time to give a rare compliment. "But I narrowed down the field today. The award for best science teamwork on a project goes to . . ."

Madison spotted Hart and Chet out of the corner of her eye. They were hoping they'd be the winners; she could tell.

"Suresh Dhir and Wayne Bronstein!"

The room filled with polite applause. Madison sank back in her seat, feeling strangely deflated.

"However." Mr. Danehy said, holding up his forefinger, "I cannot stop there. In my mind, the winners of this honor include another fine pair of my

224

students who overcame great obstacles to produce a sharp project. That's why I would like a second award to go to Madison Finn and Ivy Daly."

Thunk.

Madison was sure that her stomach had just dropped all the way to her feet. She felt clammy.

"Maddie," Aimee whispered. "He said your name. You have to go up onstage. *Now.*"

The clamminess got worse as Madison's mind raced. She had to go *where*? She was not getting on that stage. . . . She was not getting an award. . . . She was not standing next to the enemy!

Poison Ivy, meanwhile, had already worked her way up to the podium in her dumb short skirt, with her hips swinging and her red hair flipping.

Madison somehow managed to slink out of her row. Hart gave her hand a grab as she went by, which helped, but she was still pretty sure she'd fall flat on her face.

Was everyone looking at her right now?

Help.

Mere seconds had passed between the time when Mr. Danehy had made his surprise announcement and the moment Madison climbed onto the stage, but it felt like an eternity. And there was Ivy, waiting by the podium, grabbing Madison's hand and bringing her fist into the air with Ivy's own, with a wide grin, as if they were the closest of partners— and friends.

Help! Madison wanted to scream.

Instead, she leaned over to shake Mr. Danehy's hand with her free hand. He nodded approvingly. Then Madison glanced out at the crowd before her, all clapping. And then, in the middle of all the chaos, she saw Dad. He stood up in the back . . . and there was Mom, right next to him . . . and Stephanie, too . . . and Gramma Helen on the other side.

Seeing family gave Madison a lot more comfort.

"This is incredible," Madison whispered to Ivy as they stood there.

"I know," Ivy said.

"You didn't do any of the work, and you got an award," Madison said.

"No kidding," Ivy gloated.

Madison pulled her hand away and gave the enemy a hard stare. "What goes around comes around," Madison said sharply before stepping back and heading for the stage steps. "So I guess I'll see you around. . . ."

Ivy's smile disappeared in that brief exchange, but catching her enemy off guard wasn't the best revenge. As Madison walked away, Ivy wobbled just a bit on the edge of her platform shoes. That caused her to drop the award. As she bent over to retrieve it, Ivy's skirt rode up in the back. Madison saw everything, including her underwear. And so did half the assembly! As Ivy struggled to fix her outfit, she lost her balance a second time! It was the ultimate fashion malfunction for the queen of mean.

It was *perfect*.

Then Madison heard a few chuckles in the audience. She glanced back to see what the enemy had done now. Ivy stood perfectly still on the stage, frozen there like an icicle.

As she clambered back to her own seat, proudly clutching *her* award in her right hand, Madison rubbed her ear with her left hand. Dad's moonstone earrings had brought her more than luck today.

From that moment on, Madison would consider this trophy as an award not for science class or for her blue sky project, but for sheer guts.

It stood for the day when she finally took some of the air out of Ivy's sails—without sinking too far down herself to do it.

Real name   MADISON FRANCESCA FINN

Nickname   Maddie, Finnster :>)

Screen name   MadFinn

Grade @ FHJH   7th Grade GRAD!!!

Favorite class   Computer, English, and Writing

Favorite teacher   Mrs. Wing (of course)

Favorite after-school activities   The four Ws:
 Web site team (aka computer anything);
 Watching Fiona's soccer games; working
 backstage; and walking Phineas T. Finn, my pug

Hobbies   Making collages, writing in my files,
 chatting online w/my long-distance keypal,
 Bigwheels

Best achievements   Winning a prize in the
 Halloween story contest on bigfishbowl.com;
 getting the science recognition award for all of
 7th grade

Best memory   Anything with my BFFs, but
 especially these top-ten seventh-grade
 countdown moments: . . .

10. Celebrating Lindsay's 13th birthday party in
 NYC and feeling like I was with my "twin"
 sister (and shopping with Aunt Mimi on
 Madison Avenue, too, of course!)

9. Skiing Big Mountain with Aimee and surviving
 the boys, the slopes, and a really big fight

8. Making it thru Mom's reality video shoot @ FHJH—without losing my mind or all of my friends LOL

7. Babysitting 4 Eliot at the FH pool—and realizing that I can really do something if I set my mind to it

6. Making it through Dad and Stephanie's Texas wedding without a major meltdown, even when I sprained my ankle and everyone was hot and bothered and I missed home

5. Fireworks (and much more) at Gramma Helen's lake house (sigh)

4. Working in the nursing home and seeing another (good!) side of PID (code for someone who shall not be named on this Web site)

3. Winning tickets 2 a Nikki concert and realizing the truth about friendship—and how appearances can be SO deceiving

2. A big camp overnight, the bee-stinging field trip, the election Web site fiasco, and soooo many more wild times w/my class (enemies included)

1. Meeting Fiona Waters at the start of seventh grade, and finding friendship all year long with her, Aim, Madhur, and Lindsay . . . that made me laugh, cry, and wish the year would never ever end (But it has. Boo-hoo)

Chapter 18

The day after MUD, the science award, and the Ivy dismissal at school's last assembly, Madison felt as if she could breathe easier. Sure, she was worried about the upcoming clash of family members at her house, but deep down she knew that the remnants of ill will from the Big D had melted away a long time ago. Or at least, she told herself that was true. Mom's preparty tension level, however, reached an all-week high that morning.

The morning got off to a terrible start when Uncle Rick called with some bad news: Aunt Violet's tummy was on the fritz, so they would be hanging out in the hotel until she felt better. That news came around the same exact time that Phin knocked over a platter of fresh fruit that was sitting on the edge of the counter. Fortunately, Mom's painted china dish did not suffer; however, the same could not be said of the fruit salad.

As Gramma and Madison scrambled to pick up the chunks of pineapple, strawberries, and melon that were spread across the floor, Mom sat down in a kitchen chair and tried very hard not to cry.

"I should never have done this," Mom said, choking back the tears. "I'm sorry, Maddie. I should have known better. I have too much on my plate. . . ."

"Actually, Mom," Madison said, trying to make a little joke, "you have nothing on your plate . . . well, not on *this* plate anyway."

Gramma let out a little laugh, but Mom remained stone-faced.

"Mom," Madison said reassuringly as she plopped a dented berry into the sink, "things have a way of working themselves out, don't they?"

Mom shot Madison a look. "You sound like Gramma," she said.

"And that's not a bad thing, I assume," Gramma Helen said with a smile.

"Oh, Maddie," Mom sighed. She stood up and grabbed Madison in both arms. "I'm just being a nervous Nellie for no reason. It's work . . . it's having your father and aunt and uncle here . . . I don't know why I'm acting this way."

Madison wanted to say, "It's called meltdown,

Mom, and to be honest I am glad to know you have them, too." Instead, she just hugged back.

After the cleanup, Mom calmed down a lot. Madison was grateful for the fact that through it all, Gramma Helen had been there for support—for both Madison and Mom. Sometimes it *was* hard for Mom to balance all of her work and outside activities. Did Madison really take that into consideration?

It was Madison's big day, post-MUD, but she couldn't hog the limelight. Mom needed some TLC and attention today, too.

It only took another hour or so before the entire house looked—and felt—completely put together. The table was set. The food was displayed on plates and in deep bowls. The windows sparkled. Gradually, the tension began to fade—except where Phin was concerned. Phin was running on some kind of crazy energy, as if someone had pulled a cord to get him going. His little nails went, *click-click-click*, all around the house. He was probably looking for more platters to knock over, judging by the way his little pink tongue kept darting in and out of his mouth.

Pant, pant, pant.

It was some time after one o'clock when Madison looked around her living room and realized that her entire family was standing there, in one place, and that everyone was *smiling*. Even Aunt Violet was there, happy. Her sick tummy had gotten better, and she and Uncle Rick had come right over.

Dad and Stephanie stood on opposite sides of the room. Dad chatted with Gramma Helen (they'd always liked each other). Stephanie talked to Mom, which wasn't really all that weird. They seemed to be laughing like old friends. Was it possible for two people to seem so at odds and yet so compatible at the same time?

Madison smiled. Why had Mom been so worried? This was great.

Phin was the only X factor at the party. He sniffed everyone's ankles with his little pug nose and he moved from guest to guest without stopping, his curlicue tail moving in fast circles. He wasn't really begging, although he made out like a real beggar: everyone tossed scraps and cookies and crackers directly into his open mouth.

Pant, pant, yum.

At one point, Madison spotted Mom and Dad standing together, over by the buffet. They were standing very close. Too close. Dad had his hand on Mom's back. She was holding back a laugh, Madison could tell. She had her lips pursed as Dad spoke. Then Dad rubbed her back. What was going on? They seemed to lock eyes and hold hands and . . . Wait a minute!

Where was Stephanie?

Madison searched the room for her stepmother. Did Stephanie know that Mom and Dad were standing over there—that close—*talking*? Did she care?

When Madison glanced back over at Mom and Dad, she saw them embrace, warmly, as if they weren't going to let go.

"Well, hello, you."

Madison turned around and came face to face with Stephanie.

"Oh!" Madison said. "Whoa. I didn't see you there."

"Sorry about that," Stephanie said. She smiled. "I see your dad and mom are proud of you today."

Madison shrugged. "I hadn't noticed. . . ."

"They sure look proud," Stephanie said, glancing over in their direction. She stroked the side of Madison's head, pushing a strand of hair behind her ear. "And I'm very proud of you, too, Maddie. You made it through a tough year. That science award was a big wow. Did you hear your dad chanting in the audience? I couldn't shut him up."

"Aw, it wasn't *that* tough a year," Madison said.

Stephanie raised an eyebrow. "If you say so . . ."

"Well," Madison sighed. "Maybe a little tough, but just sometimes . . ."

"We're always here for you, Maddie," Stephanie said, "and when we move into the new house, things will only get better. . . ."

For some reason, Madison felt a little choked up. How could she have thought Stephanie and Dad and Mom were acting weird? The opposite was true. Even if the idea of Dad and Stephanie moving into some kind of McMansion gave Madison the heebie-jeebies.

"Maddie Finn! And Stephanie!" Gramma Helen cooed as she swept toward Madison. "What are you two gals giggling about?"

"Giggling?" Madison asked.

Stephanie laughed. "Would you excuse me? I'm going to grab Jeff for a minute."

Gramma nodded. As Stephanie walked away, Gramma took Madison's hands in hers. The skin was cool and wrinkled. Madison loved the way Gramma touched her, outside—and in.

"Some party!" Gramma said. "So why do you look blue?"

"No," Madison said. "I'm not blue! Not at all. I'm happy, actually. I was just thinking about everyone who is here. I love you all so much."

The doorbell rang, and Phin let out a howl.

"Shhhh!" Madison yelled at her dog. She hustled over to the door and flung it open. On the porch landing stood Aimee, with her dad and her dog, Blossom. The two dogs started sniffing each other hello as Aimee and her father walked inside.

"It's a big day for you two, eh?" Mr. Gillespie said.

Madison nodded. "Thanks for stopping by, Aim."

"Would I ever miss a party? My mom is coming over in a little while."

"You remember my grandma, right?" Madison asked, indicating Gramma Helen.

Madison was about to close the front door when someone ran up the porch steps. It was Madhur; her parents followed.

"You came!" Madison said.

"Duh!" Madhur said. "I promised. I don't break promises. You know that."

Madison nodded and gave her newest friend a big squeeze. "Come on in," she said, saying a quick hello to Mr. and Mrs. Singh, too.

No sooner had everyone wandered into the main part of the house than a glass was heard being clinked.

"A toast!" Mom said to the group. She raised her glass into the air. "First of all, thanks to everyone for coming to the party. It's wonderful having everyone together—*again*—in the house like this. . . ."

"Hear, hear!" Dad said.

Madison watched them shooting each other glances, just as they had in old times—only very differently. Stephanie, Gramma, and the rest of the guests cheered them along.

"I believe we have some presents for the newest soon-to-be eighth grader in our midst," Dad said.

Madison felt a little self-conscious, but she managed a wry smile. Aimee and Madhur joined her on the sofa as she opened her MUD gifts (the name Mom gave them).

The first small package was wrapped in polka-dotted paper and multicolored ribbon. The card read: *To my honey bear.* Madison knew it was from Mom.

"But you already gave me my cell phone," Madison said as she tore into the wrapping.

"Just open it," Mom said.

Inside the package was a monogrammed cell phone case, just like one Madison had seen in an issue of *Star Beat*.

"That is the coolest!" Aimee said. "It's so . . . Ivy Daly!"

Mom made a face. "Really?"

"No!" Madison scolded Aimee. "I can't believe you said that . . . right here in front of everyone. . . ."

"It's not like the drone patrol is here," Aimee said.

"Yeah," Madhur said. "Open up your next present!" She handed the next gift to Madison. This one was a lot bigger. It was wrapped in plain blue paper with a white card on top.

The note read: *For Maddie to keep smiling and filing. Love, Dad and Stephanie.*

Madison looked up at both of them and carefully tore the edge of the paper. "I have no idea what this is," she said coyly. Dad had mentioned getting Madison some new writing software and a CD burner for her laptop.

Sure enough, that was what Madison found inside the package.

The rest of the gifts on the pile were similar.

Stephanie had left Madison a bonus gift on top of the one from Dad. She had gotten Madison an enormous makeup basket and a coupon for a "day of beauty" at one of the new spa shops at the Far Hills mall. Gramma Helen's card contained a round-trip ticket to Chicago for a summer visit. Uncle Bob's and Aunt Angie's gift was right to the point: cold, hard cash. As Madison opened it, Angie winked and said, "The best gift of all." Uncle Rick and Aunt Violet gave money in their card, too. All in all, Madison made out.

After the opening of the gifts, Mom served up hot food and salad and freshly baked nut breads. Madison realized that she was hungrier than hungry. She dived in to a plate of grilled vegetables and whole wheat pasta. Her girlfriends did the same.

"Isn't Egg coming?" Aimee asked. "Or Hart? And what about Fiona?"

"They're all coming later, I think," Madison said. "I think Fiona's dad had another one of his meetings. . . ."

"Do you really think she's going to move back to California?" Madhur asked.

Madison dramatically clutched at her chest. "I hope not," she said. "What would we do without Fiona?"

"I thought more of us would be at your party," Aimee said. "What about Lindsay? She told me she'd be here."

"She's totally coming," Madison smiled. "But later—with Aunt Mimi!"

"Mimi!" Aimee let out a little chuckle. "How fabulous is that?"

"Who's Aunt Mimi?" Madhur asked.

Madison explained. "We celebrated Lindsay's thirteenth birthday this year in New York City with Aunt Mimi. She's this totally out-there, cool aunt—like the kind everybody wishes she had. She's got this huge apartment in the city, and her favorite thing to do is shop."

"Till she drops," Aimee added.

"I'm sorry I wasn't hanging out with you guys earlier this year," Madhur said. "I missed out on some of the really good stuff."

Madison threw her arm around Madhur's shoulder. "But you're here now. That's all that matters."

The family-and-friends party grew as the afternoon wore on. A few of Mom's colleagues from Budge Films came by to offer their congratulations on Madison's moving up. Although Madison knew that going from seventh grade to eighth wasn't really the biggest deal in the world, everyone made it seem like an important milestone. Madison figured that any excuse for a party made people happy. Egg would say it was the free food.

Madison wished her best guy friend was there at that moment, making fun of her as usual. She wondered if he and Mariah would come with Señora

Diaz. And she wondered whether Hart were coming. He had said probably not, that he had his own family obligations to deal with first. But he had indicated that there was still a sliver of a chance.

Mom clapped to get everyone's attention and asked a few people to dim the lights and draw the curtains. Then, with the assistance of one of the Budge Film editors, she turned on the TV. A homemade video came into view. On the screen was Madison as a little girl.

Oh, no.

Madison cringed. Mom, it seemed, had made a documentary of Madison for the party.

Help.

Luckily for Madison, it was only a three-minute video, devoted not only to her, but also to her friends. Aimee cheered at her own image up on the screen.

Strangely, Phin had calmed down with the arrival of more guests. He and Blossom stayed together, tails wagging, keeping low to the ground, where the crumbs fell. But they didn't have to beg. The guests generously gave them food, from cut-up peppers to chips and crackers. Madison knew the dogs would get stomachaches, but she didn't want to stop their fun.

By the time Mom had loaded the table with her meringue pie, cocoa cookies, and a new platter of fruit salad, the doorbell was ringing again. More guests! First, Lindsay and Aunt Mimi showed up, as promised. Aunt Mimi wore a flamboyant caftan and turban and had jewelry up and down each arm. Lindsay grabbed Madison around the waist the moment she walked inside, all hugs and tears. For some reason, she was the most emotional of the whole group of BFFs—except for Madison, of course.

Eventually, Egg, Chet, and Fiona showed up. Sadly, Mariah didn't come (she had a party at her boyfriend's house), but Madison knew she'd see more of Egg's sister over the summer. After all, she was Madison's "fill-in" big sister, too.

Egg came into the house with his obnoxiousness level set on High.

"Hey, where's the food? Where's Dan the Man?" he asked Madison. "Where's your party dress, Maddie? Where's your *boyfriend*?"

Madison pinched his arm. Aimee and Madhur each gave him a pinch, too.

"Hey! No fair! Quit pinching me!" Egg wailed.

"Oh, shut up," Fiona said. "You're such a . . ."

"Dude!" Chet cried, giving Egg a slap on the back. "We've only been here a minute, and you've already got Fiona mad at you. . . ."

Fiona crossed her arms and pouted. Across the room, a cluster of grown-ups laughed out loud. Egg turned around, as if maybe they were laughing at him.

"Paranoid?" Aimee quipped.

"When did everyone get so serious?" Egg asked. "I was only fooling around."

Fiona rolled her eyes. "Can't you just chill out? For once?"

"Hey, is Drew with you guys?" Madhur asked Egg and Chet.

"Nah," Chet answered, getting as close to Madhur as possible without standing on top of her toes. "He's got his own party going on."

"Tomorrow," Aimee said.

"Yeah, and Drew has butlers and pool guys and gardeners to do all the work! So that's no lame excuse for not being *here*."

"Chill," Fiona reminded Egg.

Egg grinned. "What? What did I say? I'm totally chill. Man, I'm an ice cube."

Everyone had to smile. No matter how annoying he became, Egg usually got the last laugh.

Bzzzzzzzzzzzzzzzzzzzzzzz.

Something rumbled in Madison's pocket. Her cell phone was set to VIBRATE. Madison lifted it out and read the display. It read HJ.

Hart was calling her right now!

Madison scrambled to punch the right key and pick up the call, but the phone stopped ringing. A moment later, TEXT MESSAGE flashed on the display. Madison retrieved the message.

Where r u? I'm @ this family thing w/Drew . . .

Madison smiled. So *that's* where they were. She'd nearly forgotten. Hart and Drew were cousins. Usually, their families celebrated a lot of the holidays and big events together. Big events like MUD.

She kept reading. It was a long message.

I can't wait 2 c u @ the pool thing 2morrow. BUT I need to really talk 2 u about something v.v. important ok? It's kind of a big deal ok? C u l8r g8r. xo H.

Madison couldn't wipe the smile off her face when she read the last part. Hart never *ever* signed a note or a text message with an X or O. That meant he was sending her a hug *and* kiss. A kiss! He was getting serious.

But then Madison went back to the other part of the message—the part about needing to talk, *really* talk. What did that mean? Her curiosity was piqued. What could be so important? Why hadn't he given her any better clues?

"Maddie!" Fiona came over and grabbed Madison's elbow. "I think a bunch of us are talking about going down to the lake in a while. My mom was just talking to your mom about giving everyone a ride. Go grab your suit in case we jump in."

"Wait. We're all going *swimming*?" Madison asked. "But tomorrow is the pool party."

"So?" Fiona said. "It's hot outside. Let's go swim. It's not like we can't swim two days in a row, silly."

"Nah, I can't," Madison shook her head. "I have to help my mom clean up all the food and the dishes," Madison said.

The truth was, her mind was elsewhere. She was still thinking about Hart's text message.

"Maddie?" Fiona gave her a little punch. "This may be one of the last times that we all hang out as seventh graders. . . . Your mom gets it. . . . She just told my mom that we should *all* go . . . and that means you, too. . . ."

"What do you mean, one of the last times we all hang out?" Madison asked.

Hold on. She didn't like the sound of *that*. Was Fiona implying that maybe one of them would be gone over the summer? Was it Fiona herself who would be gone? As in, *moving* gone?

All at once Madison's mind was at full tilt, programmed to *overthink*.

"Okay, okay, fine . . . I guess I could go," Madison said slowly, "since you're twisting my arm . . ."

"Maybe Hart and Drew will even show up," Fiona said, leaning across to really twist Madison's arm.

"Ouch!" Madison cried out playfully. "I'll go. I'll go."

Madison glanced around the room again. Gramma and Mom were over in one corner, picking up a few cups and plates. Uncles Rick and Bob were chatting with Dad. Stephanie and Aunt Violet were in some deep discussion with Madhur's mother. Madison felt safe there, right now, surrounded by all those people that mattered to her.

But she felt something else, too.

All through seventh grade, Madison had grown accustomed to expecting the unexpected, but was it possible that this time around, the unexpected could spell trouble, instead of pleasant surprises, for her? Something told her that the moment she left the party, things could—and would—change.

With a deep breath, Madison told her friends to wait while she headed upstairs to get her things. She was going to need a lot more than her moonstone earrings to survive the postgraduation party scene.

Chapter 19

The morning of Drew's pool party was the sunniest—and hottest—June day on record in Far Hills. Luckily, the air conditioner at 5 Blueberry Street blasted cool air through Madison's bedroom. She rolled over onto her blankets, reached for her laptop, and powered it up.

A Little Bit of Luck

Talk about relieved. The party did NOT continue @ the lake yesterday. The sun just vanished and these thick clouds moved in so fast, cool and creepy @ the same time, like that movie *Twister*. We decided it was

better 2 just hang on my porch where we
played Monopoly for about twenty minutes
until Egg declared he was bored stiff. He
and Chet and Madhur went into Mom's office
to play some killer video game. The rest of
us stayed outside gossiping. I thought I
saw Rose Thorn walk by (she lives close to
me) but maybe it was this other girl who
goes to private school. I think her name
is Edith or something old-fashioned. Who
knows? There are a lot of new people
moving in everywhere. I guess it makes
sense, since so many other peeps are
moving away.

I love this feeling of waking up in AC,
buried under the comforter. I know Phinnie
loves it, too. But he's been acting so
strange since the party. I think he ate too
much people food. Sometimes I am convinced
that Phin thinks he's a person and not a
pooch.

I've been racking my brain trying to
think about what Hart could possibly have 2
say 2 me @ Drew's party 2day. He's never
secretive like this. Maybe he wants to
confess his true love for Ivy! HA! HA! HA!
Hold on while I pee laughing.

I've decided that I need 2 look as hot
as possible 4 this party. First of all,
seventh grade is over (whoa) and that means
eighth grade is coming and I need to try a
little harder. LOL. Second, I have 2 do it
4 Hart, of course. But I also have to look

good b/c everyone will be taking loads of photos. Note to self: I do not want 2 go down in history as former seventh grader AND style reject.

Rude Awakening: Gramma Helen always says a little luck can go a long way on the path to happiness. But I don't need to go *that* far. Just from here to Drew's place and back again. Is that so much to ask for?

I better run. Aim's waiting and we're supposed 2 be over @ Fiona's in half an hour. Her dad is giving us the ride to the party. Maybe when we're w/them, he or F's mom will spill the beans about a big move back 2 California? I wonder. Someone has to admit something sooner or later, right? They can't go on pretending like there isn't some big change a-coming.

Phin danced through the piles of clothes on Madison's bedroom floor. First, jeans; then, a peasant skirt; and finally, a pair of lemon-colored capris, upon which Madison finally decided, even though she considered the possibility that they might get dirty. When it came to clothes and shoes, there was always so much to consider.

The phone rang.

"Madison!" Mom called out. "Aimee wants to know if you're coming or not!"

"I'm coming! I'm coming!"

Madison scrambled to pull on the capris and a

T-shirt with flowers across the front. As she quickly slid on a pair of tan-colored sandals with toe loops, Phin started licking her feet. He always figured out how to get in the way when Madison was in a super rush.

Finally, she was ready to go. Madison held open her orange bag (currently empty) and tossed in all of the "essentials" that had been piled on her bed: tankini and bottoms; pink pool flip-flops; SpongeBob SquarePants beach towel (the only towel she could find); SPF 45+ sunscreen; Far Hills Rangers visored cap; LifeSavers (butterscotch and winter-green); digital camera (still on loan from Dad); an extra T-shirt that matched the capris; amazing cat-eyed sunglasses that she'd gotten while shopping with Mom the week before; and a Hello Kitty wallet, even though she wouldn't need money, because, of course, Drew's parents always supplied *everything*.

With an on-the-run kiss for both Mom and Phin, Madison flung the bag over her shoulder and raced to Aimee's house. Her BFF was standing on the porch in her own summer ensemble: peach-colored bikini top; woven leather flip-flops; and rainbow striped miniskirt (which was actually more like a skort).

"I thought you'd never get here!" Aimee sighed when she saw Madison. She picked up her straw bag and slid it under her arm. "Are you ready? Fiona called me, like, five minutes ago."

"I'm sorry," Madison said. She felt a little winded

after all of her hurrying. "I lost track of time this morning."

The two of them rushed over to the Waterses' house. Mr. Waters was on the porch with a pile of cardboard boxes he was taping together.

"Hey, Mr. Waters!" Aimee called out.

"What's going on?" Madison asked as they got closer to the front door.

"Oh, *this*?" Mr. Waters groaned. He lifted up one box. "Too much stuff. We're cleaning house."

"Oh," Madison said.

Aimee nudged Madison gently. "Let's go inside, Maddie."

The two strolled through the screen door and called for their friend. "Fiona!"

Fiona appeared in denim shorts, Keds, and a cutoff T-shirt with the words SOCCER ROCKS on the front. She had her braids pulled into elastic bands in back. It was her hairstyle when the weather was steamy.

"I thought you'd never get here!" Fiona said.

"That sounds familiar," Madison sighed. "Aimee just said the same thing to me. It's my fault."

"Who cares?" Fiona said. "I just wanted to have a few minutes with you before we head over to the party. We have the hugest news. And I know, Maddie, that I promised I would tell you if anything changed. . . ."

Changed?

250

"Like what?" Madison asked, nervous about what she was going to hear.

"Does this have to do with your move?" Aimee asked.

"What move?" Fiona asked, confused. "You mean to California?"

Madison and Aimee nodded at the same time.

"I think you'd better ask my mom for the details," Fiona said.

Madison couldn't understand how Fiona could be smiling at a time like that. They followed her into the kitchen.

Inside, there were more boxes piled up by the sink and counter. Mrs. Waters was wrapping dishes in bubble wrap.

"Maddie! Aimee!" Mrs. Waters cheered as soon as she saw Fiona's friends. "So, today's the big pool party at Drew's, huh? Sounds like a lot of fun."

"Any party at Drew's place is a hoot," Aimee replied.

"Mom, I told Maddie and Aim that we have news," Fiona said.

"Oh, you did?" Mrs. Waters said.

"I think I already know what it is," Madison said quietly.

"You do?" Mrs. Waters answered. "That's surprising. I thought we Waterses were good at keeping secrets. But it makes sense. . . ."

Fiona reached out and grabbed her mom's hand.

"You tell them, Fiona," Mrs. Waters said.

Madison bit her lip, waiting. Aimee looked a little worried now, too. All signs seemed to indicate that a big move was coming. First, thought Madison, it had been the dad meetings, and now it was boxes and packing tape. . . .

"I'm going to be a big sister!" Fiona cried.

Madison and Aimee did a double take.

"What?" they said at the exact same time.

"Mom and Dad are having another baby!" Fiona said again.

Madison's stomach did a loop de loop. She couldn't believe her ears. Mrs. Waters was pregnant?

"I'm just grateful that it's one baby and not another set of twins," Mrs. Waters joked.

Everyone laughed.

"A baby! Duh! Of course!" Aimee said, trying to play smart even though she hadn't ever considered this.

"So, let me get this straight. . . . You're *not* moving?" Madison asked Mrs. Waters.

Fiona's mom shook her head gently. "No, of course we're not moving. Whatever gave you that idea?"

Madison climbed up onto one of the stools in the Waterses' kitchen and put her face in her hands. "I guess I just assumed . . . when Mr. Waters was interviewing with all those people in California and . . . all the boxes . . ."

"No, no," Mrs. Waters said. "I can see how you jumped to conclusions. We're remodeling the kitchen and Fiona's dad has been looking for an alternative position."

"Sounds like my mom," Madison said. "She was thinking of changing jobs, too."

"There must be something going around," Mrs. Waters said.

"I would have told you if I knew for sure we were moving, Maddie! I said that to you, like, a hundred times," Fiona said.

"Yeah," Madison admitted, blushing a little. "I guess I worried for nothing."

"So, do you know what this means?" Aimee asked the group.

Madison and Fiona smiled as Aimee told them.

"We'll be together for eighth grade, just like we always planned!"

"Hooray!"

Aimee and Madison huddled around Fiona inside the kitchen. It was an ideal time for a BFF clinch—or at least a quick hug. They had to get moving if they were going to make it to Drew's party in time for the action.

Of course, it wasn't all about the pool or the BBQ for Madison. She was mostly eager to see Hart and to hear *his* big news.

Mr. Waters drove the girls and Chet down the long

driveway in front of Drew's house. As always, Mrs. Maxwell stood at the steps ready to greet the guests. She had on a pair of sunglasses that were much too big for her face, but that made her look like a movie star.

"Hello, hello!" Mrs. Maxwell called out to all of Drew's friends and their parents as they approached. "Hurry inside. The show is about to begin!"

"The *show*?" Aimee repeated. "Is she kidding?"

"I think she just means the *party*," Fiona said.

"Who cares?" Chet cried. "Let's go. I wanna find Egg and the guys."

Madison adjusted the waistband on her lemon capris and followed behind the others into Drew's yard. She kept her eyes peeled for Hart.

When they got to the backyard, Madison gasped. Mrs. Maxwell hadn't been joking. It really did look like a show. It reminded Madison of the final scene in the movie *Grease*, where all the kids go to a huge outdoor carnival with rides and concession stands— only, this was taking place in someone's backyard.

Crazy.

"Is this for real?" Aimee asked. "Drew's parents usually go way over the top, but this is like a Hollywood movie set or something."

"Check that out!" Fiona said. "Jugglers!"

"And that clown over there is making balloon animals. Oh, let's go . . . I want to get one. . . ." Aimee said, tugging on the back of Madison's T-shirt.

In addition to the juggler and balloon man, the yard contained a dunking tank and a cotton candy machine. Madison recalled the start-of-school party, when Mrs. Maxwell had put out tiki torches everywhere. This time around, she had bunches of balloons and blow-up palm trees. Aimee was right on the mark: this was overkill—*plus*.

"Hey, you guys!" Drew said, appearing in his bathing trunks. He had on a tank top and three leis.

"Your mom has lost it," Aimee joked. "This is incredible!"

"I know, I know," Drew said, bowing his head in mock embarrassment. "I said, 'Hey, Ma, what if we just barbecued some dogs and had cans of soda and went swimming?' She thought I was kidding. That's when she hired all the clowns. And I don't know about you guys, but clowns freak me out."

Madison laughed. "Juggling clowns with squirting flowers on their lapels aren't so bad," she teased.

Drew laughed back, even though he was probably not amused in the least. "Egg, Dan, and Hart are already here. They're over there playing Ping-Pong, I think. Or maybe they went swimming. . . ."

Madison glanced around but didn't see the guys anywhere.

"No way!" Aimee blurted out.

Drew looked concerned. "What? What's the matter?"

255

"Drew, you are the biggest dorkus on the planet," Aimee said.

"Aim!" Madison scolded. "Why would you say something like that? Drew is our friend, and he invited us to come here and—"

"Maddie, look who's here," Aimee said, interrupting.

Madison turned to look. *Ivy Daly stood a few yards away. And she was with the drones.*

"Dre-e-e-e-e-e-ew," Madison groaned. "You invited *Ivy*?"

Drew shrugged his shoulders. "My mother invited every member of our class. I didn't have a say. Sorry. She said it wasn't nice to leave people out."

"That's what they tell you in nursery school," Fiona said. "'Make sure you invite everyone from the class.' But the rules change a lot by the time junior high rolls around, don't you think?"

Drew looked despondent. "I knew you girls would give me a hard time about having Poison Ivy here. Just blow her off. Who cares?"

Madison was ready to explode.

Who cares? Was he kidding? How could you blow off something that slimy?

Just then, Lindsay and Madhur came over together.

"This party is the atomic bomb," Madhur said. "Did any of you guys try one of Drew's dad's fruit smoothies yet? There's a clown over there who makes them to order. Amazing."

"Maddie, you look pretty today," Lindsay said, giving Madison a warm smile. "Dressing special for anyone in particular?"

Aimee chuckled. "Like we don't know who!"

"For Dan, of course," Fiona teased.

"Dan?" Madison asked, confused.

"Hey," Lindsay said, giving Fiona a little pinch. "Dan's mine."

"But you do mean Pork-O, don't you?" Aimee cracked.

Fiona made a face. "Stop being mean," she warned Aimee. "He doesn't deserve that nickname anymore."

"When he stops stealing brownies off lunch trays, I'll ditch the name," Aimee said. "But until then—"

"Let's just go find the other guys," Madison suggested. "And do everything in our power to avoid the enemy, okay?"

The cluster of BFFs marched across the lawn toward their other guy friends. Madison figured that Ivy probably saw her, but as long as Madison didn't make eye contact, things would be just dandy.

"Is Ben coming?" Aimee wondered aloud.

Madhur giggled. "I can't believe you have such a crush. I mean, did you hear that speech yesterday? He's the biggest brainiac ever."

"Look who's talking, Madhur!" Aimee said.

"You're the one who likes *Chet*. I mean, that takes the cake."

"What cake?" Madhur said.

"Stop talking about cake," Lindsay cut in. "It's making me hungry."

Madison couldn't believe her friends were bickering—and about these boys. Then again, she'd been bitten by the boy bug recently, too.

"Yo! Over here!" Egg saw the girls coming and waved.

Fiona raced over first. Then, as expected, Madhur went straight up to Chet. Lindsay found Dan, too. Hart smiled at Madison.

Aimee looked momentarily lost, with no specific boy destination, but the lost look lasted only a few seconds. Madison figured that Ben probably wasn't coming, and most girls would have wilted hearing that kind of news, but Aimee didn't appear to let it get her down. Then again, she was never one to let boys get her down.

Like right now.

Aimee smoothed out her shirt and struck a confident dancer's pose.

"Know what this party needs?" Aimee declared. "Good music. Hey, Drew!" She called out for their friend and left the couples behind.

Madison admired the way Aimee didn't need anyone else to tell her how to act or what to believe or how to feel—even when she was the odd girl out.

She was always opinionated and straightforward and so . . . well, so *Aimee*. That made her all the more lovable.

Hold on.

Madison stopped in midthought and blinked. What was she thinking? Where was her head? Talk about a sentimentality overdose.

Bleccch.

Of all people *not* to get overmushy about, Aimee led the list. If Aimee had known what Madison had just been thinking, she would probably have made little sick faces and stuck out her tongue like a grass snake. . . .

Okay, back to reality.

Madison's thoughts whizzed from Aimee to their little group to the clown juggler and back again, trying to find another reality landing strip somewhere in Drew's backyard. What was it about this whole scene that felt like a movie set, besides *everything*?

Just then, a clown with an enormous red nose and oversize green shoes waddled over toward Madison and sprayed her with some Silly String.

Her friends laughed. Hart was the loudest. Madison watched them clutch their stomachs, laughing all the while.

"What's so funny?" Madison asked innocently as she plucked string out of her hair.

Chet was practically rolling on the lawn. Then Drew came back over, with his mother by his side.

"Nice clowns," Madison said.

"Aw, darling!" Mrs. Maxwell said as she pulled a strand of string off Madison's shoulder. "I don't think it'll stain your shirt."

"Sorry," Drew said, stifling one of his usual snort-laughs. Through the entire seventh-grade year he had continuously snorted.

"It's okay," Madison said. "I'll get you back."

"What's the next attraction, Drew?" Lindsay asked.

Drew threw his arms up in the air. "Karaoke!" he declared. "We set up a machine in the screening room."

Madison and her friends exchanged smiles. They'd all been over a few times during the school year to watch videos and nosh on flavored popcorn. It was like watching a movie in your own private theater; it was certainly better than renting movies at the store and watching them on a thirty-two-inch TV set like the one in Madison's living room.

Aimee raced toward the screening room with Madison, Madhur, Fiona, and Lindsay right behind her. But they weren't the only girls headed that way. Ivy and her drones walked just ahead.

How perfect.

"Hey, Finnster, hold up!"

Hart was right on Madison's heels. She turned to face him.

"Where's the fire?" he joked.

Madison smiled. "I can't believe Poison Ivy is here *with* her drones."

Hart chuckled. "Yeah, crazy. Right?"

The other boys walked past, leaving Madison and Hart alone on a patch of grass. Everyone else was karaoke-bound.

"We should go," Madison said, turning back around again. But Hart grabbed her elbow.

"Can we talk?" Hart asked.

Madison nodded. "Sure."

He sounded so serious.

"I mean, *really* talk. I mean . . . well . . . I have to tell you something important."

"What's going on?" Madison asked. "Is this the thing you texted me about yesterday?"

"Yeah."

"Is something the matter? Are you feeling okay?"

"Not really."

Madison got a lump in her throat.

"What's the matter?" she asked Hart.

By now, everyone had pretty much disappeared into the house. Madison saw that the only people left outside were her, Hart, and the clown with all the balloon animals. He was working on a giraffe with a very long, orange neck.

"Look," Hart stammered. "I don't know how to tell you this. . . ."

The lump in Madison's throat multiplied tenfold.

She did *not* like the sound of this. The conversation sounded like one of those soap opera scenes right before the girl gets ditched. All sorts of questions blazed through her mind. Here they were at the end of seventh grade. It made sense that it could be the end of something else, too. Was Hart planning to like Ivy instead? Was there some girl he lifeguarded with at the pool? Had he decided that he'd rather stay "just friends" with Madison instead of staying "in like" with her?

"I have some news . . . well, *bad* news . . ." Hart said. "I mean, I think it stinks so much."

"Stinks?" Madison's eyes got wide. "What is it?" she asked.

As Hart ran his fingers through his brown, tousled hair, Madison noticed a row of freckles near his ear that she'd never noticed before. She stared at him—hard—and listened close, wanting to reach out and touch those freckles. But she kept her hands to herself.

"Just tell me what it is," Madison said softly.

She expected Hart to launch into some long-winded explanation, but he didn't. He didn't say a word. Instead, Hart leaned very close to Madison's face, so close that she could practically see his pores.

A few moments passed.

"Um . . . *Hart*?"

"Madison?"

"Hart?" Madison said his name a second time.

What was he doing?

All at once, without warning, Hart leaned forward a little more, right into Madison. He pressed his face into her face, kind of hard, so that their teeth clicked together.

He was kissing her.

Kissing her! Kissing her!

This wasn't like the other few kisses Madison and Hart had shared that seventh-grade year, either; those had been quick pecks or near misses. This kiss lasted at least ten glorious seconds. Madison was very glad to be wearing her favorite strawberry-kiwi lip gloss just then. Her heart raced like a stopwatch.

"Why did you do that?" she asked.

"Because," Hart said. "Why not?"

For a brief moment, Madison thought Hart might take her into his arms with another sweeping gesture and kiss her even harder, until her lips went numb, the way they always did whenever she ate Popsicles.

But there was no follow-up kiss.

Instead, they both started to laugh.

Chapter 20

"So that's what you wanted to tell me? *That's* the bad news?" Madison said, still catching her breath. She licked her lips. The gloss was gone.

"Well, that's not exactly what I wanted to say. . . ." Hart mumbled. He had stopped laughing.

Madison's eyes darted around the yard, but other than the clowns (and, really, who cared about the clowns anymore?), they were alone. In the distance, Madison could hear a drumbeat. Everyone was off doing karaoke.

Hart rubbed his mouth. It looked a little as if he were wiping off the kiss, as a four-year-old would do, but Madison didn't care. Her head was somewhere way up in the clouds.

She wanted him to kiss her again.

"You know, I like you," Hart said simply.

Madison nodded. "I know. Seventh grade has been the coolest year ever, and I like you, too."

"But I'm so bummed out," Hart said.

Madison looked at Hart quizzically and then looked away. There was something in his eyes, something sad.

"Why are you bummed?"

"Maddie, my parents just told me something this week. . . ."

Hart looked away. Madison didn't speak. She waited for him to finish.

"We're moving," Hart blurted out.

"Moving on up?" Madison said, giggling at first. Then she realized Hart was serious.

"Wait. You're *really* moving?" Madison cocked her head to one side and looked Hart squarely in the eye. "But why? Wait! Don't tell me . . . your dad got a job transfer. . . ."

"How did you know that?" Hart said, looking at Madison with narrowed eyes. "Seriously, how did you know?"

"Everyone's changing jobs, it seems," Madison groaned. "It's like the chicken pox or something."

"Huh?"

"So, what about the summer?" Madison asked.

"I dunno. We're leaving in three weeks. For Europe," Hart said.

"You're moving to Europe? That's so far away. . . ."

"Dad and Mom need to get over there, they said. We just put our Far Hills house on the market. Dad needs to meet with some people at his new gig."

"What about lifeguarding at the pool this summer?" Madison asked.

"Well, obviously I won't be doing that. . . ." Hart said.

"But you just told me the other day . . ." Madison started to say. Her voice quavered.

Of course he wouldn't be doing that. Duh.

"My parents didn't really fill me in until this week," Hart admitted. "Then they made this big announcement at the graduation party yesterday. I was out of the loop—way out of the loop—before that."

"Does Drew know?" Madison asked.

Hart nodded. "Yeah, Drew knows. But you know him. He's Mr. Easygoing."

"Europe? Wow," Madison said. For a split second, she had a mental image of Hart standing under the Eiffel Tower; Madison walked up to him in her imagined scene and took his hands and began speaking French while wearing a little blue beret and eating a baguette.

"You can come visit me there if you want," Hart suggested.

"Yeah," Madison said. "If I win the lottery. Otherwise, I guess we have to remain long-distance . . ."

"Why don't you come with your mom when she goes over to do work on some documentary?"

"She isn't going to Europe this year," Madison said. "This summer, she's off to Japan. Why don't you move to Tokyo instead?"

Hart grinned. "No problem. Let me just call my dad and tell him."

Madison reached for Hart's hand.

"You can't leave," Madison said. "Not now. What about eighth grade?"

Hart shrugged. "I know. But at least we can always e-mail."

They both stared into each other's eyes—and then away again—off in opposite directions. As they stood there, a few kids came back out onto the lawn. Madison saw Aimee and Madhur out of the corner of her eye.

"Maddie!" they called from across the lawn. Soon, all the party guests were returning from the karaoke. Apparently the game was not as fun as being out in the backyard.

A moment later, Hart went off with Chet and a few other boys. He didn't really say good-bye. The private moment was over.

It wasn't the only thing that was over.

Madison tried to hide her disappointment from her friends. But that was a lost cause. Of course, they could tell something was wrong right away. BFFs have special radar for that sort of thing.

"Wait! Did you tell Hart about *Will*?" Aimee whispered to Madison.

"No!" Madison said. "No way."

"Then what happened? You guys disappeared, and we all went inside. Drew didn't even realize you were gone, and then he stopped the karaoke and I was looking for you. . . ."

Fiona was babbling. She hardly ever babbled, which meant that just then she was truly worried about Madison.

"Fiona, I'm okay," Madison said, trying to reassure her.

"Maddie," Lindsay said, hugging her friend. "Are you *really* okay?"

"Because you look really *not* okay," Madhur said.

Madison could feel all the emotion in her belly, pressing from the inside out. With Hart's bad news, seventh grade had just come to its real screeching halt.

"I'll be okay eventually," Madison said, thereby admitting that perhaps she wasn't one hundred percent fine. "It's just that . . . Hart told me his family is moving away from Far Hills."

Madison's friends all gasped.

"And you thought *we* were moving," Fiona said. "That's terrible. Hart's moving? Oh, Maddie, I am so, so, *so* sorry. . . ."

"You can have a long-distance relationship, can't you?" Madhur said.

Madison frowned. "I guess. But everyone says those things don't work."

"Seriously, it can! You can text-message and e-mail and visit on school vacations and . . ." Lindsay was trying to be upbeat, but it wasn't really working.

"He's moving to Europe," Madison said flatly.

For a moment no one said a word. Maybe long-distance *was* out of the question.

"Well," Madison finally said. "I'll live."

"You'll *live*?" Aimee shot back. "How? Maddie, you're talking about the guy you've crushed on forever. You're talking about Hart Jones!"

Madison covered her mouth. Aimee was right. This was a bigger than big deal. But she didn't want to cry.

So now what?

The only thing capable of holding back her tears was a very strong dam. So everyone pressed together in a group hug. No sooner had everyone huddled together than they heard a loud "Puh-leeze!" from nearby.

There was Ivy, flanked by her drones.

Madison stepped back with her arms crossed in front of her. Her friends did the same. Now they really looked like a dam, ready to block anything—especially the enemy.

"Back off," said Aimee.

Ivy started to laugh. "Oh, like I'm so scared of you guys," she said.

"You should be," Madhur said.

"As if!" Rose Thorn snapped. She and Phony Joanie stepped forward a bit. For a moment, Madison thought they might actually get into a real fight.

"Look . . ." Madison started to say.

Ivy interrupted. "No, you look. Seventh grade may be over, but we are so not over, Madison Finn. . . ."

"Remember what you said to me a few weeks ago, Ivy?" Madison interjected. "About how I would never be the class star . . ."

"And I was so-o-o-o right," Ivy huffed.

"Well . . . uh . . . you know . . . stars *fade*," Madison said. She wanted to say something cleverer, but she couldn't think of anything.

Drat.

"Um, did you just say stars *fade*?" Phony Joanie grunted. "Good one, Madison."

The drones and Ivy looked at one another and laughed.

"I don't know why you're laughing, Ivy," Aimee said. "That was a real 'star' move up there on stage at assembly yesterday. . . ."

Ivy looked instantly embarrassed. She smoothed down her skirt as if she were remembering what had happened up there at MUD.

"Hey, what's going on over here?" Drew asked. He had appeared, wearing a black magician's cape, carrying a top hat and wand. "You're going to miss my show."

Ivy and the drones finally backed away, rolling their eyes.

The rest of Drew's party was fun and games, and a spectacle—as usual. A couple of the clowns did an acrobatic act, jumping around on a trampoline. After they finished, the party guests got a turn on the trampoline, too.

Madison, Fiona, Aimee, Madhur, and Lindsay decided to jump at the same time, holding hands. At one point, Fiona's knees locked. It was a chain reaction: the five friends tumbled down at the same time.

"Attention!" Mrs. Maxwell's voice boomed across the lawn. "Time for lunch, kids!"

Madison and the others hopped off the trampoline and headed for a large tent set up at the side of the Maxwell lawn. On a pair of tables was a buffet fit for a king, queen, and half of an entire kingdom: hamburgers, hot dogs, fifteen kinds of salad, fresh fruit, rolls, cookies, and much more. Eyes and mouths watered at the sight of the spread. Kids dived in with forks, spoons, and fingers. Just when it seemed as if Mrs. Maxwell had served up more than anyone could have dreamed, a couple of clowns rolled onto the lawn with a cart, to make personalized ice-cream sundaes.

"Check it out!" Drew said. "It's a portable Freeze

271

Palace!" he cried, referring to their favorite ice-cream spot in Far Hills.

Kids clambered for the hot-fudge brownie blast and cookies-and-cream explosion, two special recipes prepared expressly for the seventh-grade grads. Madison noticed that Ivy and the drones stayed as far away from her as possible.

Music blared from speakers on the Maxwell patio; the party went a lot longer than anyone expected.

Mrs. Maxwell didn't seem to mind one bit. She floated from one group of kids to the next, serving more cans of soda and little bags of popcorn. Everyone was getting stuffed.

And it was getting late. The clock said five o'clock.

Madison and Hart had found time to hang out together more after their big talk, but neither of them mentioned Hart's moving again.

That was a very good thing.

Madison knew that once the idea of Hart's leaving really sank in, she would turn into a water-works—and she certainly didn't want to do it there in front of the whole ex-seventh-grade class. She would have to save all her tears and also her good-byes for much later, over the phone, in person, and via e-mail. She'd think of a million other ways to tell Hart how much she would miss him. After all, who would call her Finnster from then on?

"Hey, Maddie." Aimee came up beside Madison as they were all getting ready to leave Drew's house. "I was thinking maybe you could come up on the roof with me. Fiona said she'd come, too."

"What about Lindsay and Madhur?"

"They have to go home with their parents," Aimee explained.

"So, it's just the three of us?" Madison asked.

"The original musketeers," Aimee said, spinning around with a savvy dance move on the grass. She really could twirl anywhere.

Fiona's dad picked them up in front of the mansion. Chet didn't go back with them, though. He'd decided to head over to Egg's to play video games for a couple of hours and eat dinner with Egg's family.

On the ride home, Madison gazed out of the window of the Waterses' van, watching the streets and parks and stores of Far Hills pass by. It seemed hard to believe that so much could change in such a short time.

Madison saw a blond boy outside. He was riding his bike through an intersection, and for a fleeting moment, Madison thought maybe it was Will again. Of course, it wasn't him. Will was nowhere near Far Hills just then. Madison wondered if she ever would see him again. Now that Hart was going to move away . . .

Stop overthinking. One day at a time.

By the time everyone got dropped off at Aimee's

273

house, it was six o'clock: dinnertime. Mrs. Gillespie told Mr. Waters that she'd "feed the troops" and that Fiona could spend the night, too. She called Madison's mom, too, and asked permission to let Madison join the dinner and sleepover.

Madison and Fiona knew the invitation was a mixed blessing. It meant being served some kind of vegan, macrobiotic food, but that was okay. They'd already stuffed themselves with pigs-in-blankets, popcorn, and ice cream all day. A little brown rice and tempeh burgers wouldn't be so bad on a junk-food tummy. Besides, the sleepover was the more important part of the night.

Aimee's four brothers were all home for dinner that night; and they proceeded to tease Aimee and her friends mercilessly throughout the meal about being "dorky girls." It wasn't mean-spirited, however, and no one minded their barbs. For Aimee, of course, this was a nightly occurrence. For Fiona, too, it was second nature. After all, she lived with Chet. Although Madison had no brothers of her own, she'd gotten used to being teased after spending so much time with the four Gillespie brothers, Egg, and her other guy friends at school. In many ways, Madison Francesca Finn was *not* an only child. Not by a long shot.

After supper, Aimee led her friends up to her bedroom. She opened the window and screen and invited Madison and Fiona to climb out onto her rooftop. The air was balmy, with just a light breeze. Outside it smelled like charcoal from barbecues people were having that night in the neighborhood. Aimee sprayed insect repellent on everyone's arms so the mosquitoes wouldn't get them as the sun went down. Then she lit a citronella candle and they sat in a circle together.

Although it was past eight o'clock by then, it was still light outside. Madison, Aimee, and Fiona stared off at the clouds, waiting for night to come.

"So, what else did Hart say?" Aimee asked after a while.

Madison shrugged. "Not much. Uh . . . can we *not* talk about him?"

"Yeah," Fiona said gently. "Let's not talk about boys at all."

"Who needs boys?" Aimee said.

Madison knew that Ben's not having shown up for Drew's party was another good reason for avoiding the boy talk. She knew Aimee was probably feeling down in the dumps a little bit herself.

"The only really dependable people in the whole universe . . ." Fiona started to say.

". . . are girlfriends," Madison finished. "Duh!"

Aimee smiled. "Hey, look! The moon is coming out, and it isn't even dark yet. I love that."

Way up in the sky, a round, white orb dangled between two clouds. But it wasn't just any moon. That night it would be a full moon.

275

The "three musketeers" sat together as the sky turned darker blue, their faces illuminated by the flicker of the candle, the faint glow of the lights on the street below, and the lamp inside Aimee's bedroom. Although they probably could have sat talking on the roof for hours about Hart, Ivy, and the promise of eighth grade, Madison and her two friends didn't say much at all. Maybe it was because they were tired. After all, it had been a long day at Drew's party, and an even longer week at school.

Madison thought of something Gramma Helen had said one time.

"I know you're going to think I sound like a peanutty cluster," Gramma Helen had mused, using one of her kookier expressions, "but people who love each other know one thing best: how to sit quietly together. Oftentimes, they know what the other person is thinking without even having to ask. One of the best parts of being a best friend is just 'being.'"

As she remembered those words, Madison glanced at Aimee and then over at Fiona. Both of her friends gazed up at the stars in the darkening sky.

Madison's thoughts raced. Where would the three of them be this time next year? What about the year after that? What boys would they know? What enemies would they face together? Where would they travel? What secrets would they share?

As Madison sat asking herself a zillion questions, she was sure the moment of silence wouldn't last. Aimee would start talking, and then Fiona would join in, and then the three of them would sit there mocking Poison Ivy or a Far Hills teacher or complaining about the latest issue of *Star Beat*.

But that wasn't what happened.

Aimee didn't say anything. Neither did Fiona. They just sat there, wordless.

One of the best parts of being a best friend is just "being."

In that moment, that quieter-than-quiet moment, Madison knew something deep in her heart.

This friendship was the real thing.

And these three would be friends till the end of everything.

Mad Chat Words:

W^?	What's up?
DTS?	Doesn't that stink?
9ML8R	Call me later
+:>)	Putting on my thinking cap
WBSTS	Write back sooner than soon
LTNE-M	Long time no e-mail
LMKWYT	Let me know what you think
HAY?	How are you?
IMU	I miss you
NSL	No such luck
W2US	Write to you soon
SUS	See you soon
{:->}	Happy/doofy face
**>	Blushing with stars in my eyes
DCTS	Don't change the subject
:>Pffft	Oh, no!
WEIN?	What else is new?
Gesswat?	Guess what?
((U))	Hugging you

Madison's Computer Tip

Whether you have a laptop, a PC, a cell phone, or whatever, **find new, smart, and safe ways to stay connected with all the people you care about**. Sometimes you don't need to leave a long message. You can just say HIYA or HEY, or you could ask a bunch of cool questions (kind of like Mrs. Wing's memory pages) and get the inside scoop. Being good @ the computer takes a lot of time (to learn stuff); discipline (knowing your Netiquette inside and out); and creativity. You have all of that—and much more. GL online—and off. :>)

For a complete Mad Chat dictionary and more about Madison Finn, visit Madison at www.lauradower.com

Like Madison Finn, author Laura Dower is an only child, enjoys her laptop computer, and drinks root beer. Laura has written more than seventy books for kids. She lives in New York with her husband and three children.

Visit Laura at www.lauradower.com

From the Files of Madison Finn

VIN*! There's 25 LOL funny books in the Madison Finn series!!

WAYG2D*? Collect them all!

*: Very Important News
*WAYG2D: What Are You Going 2 Do